Separate T~

Jane Rogers was born in Londo~
moved frequently, so she atte~
schools, including two in New Y~
English at Cambridge, and traine~
Leicester University. She has wor~ ~ildren's
home, for a housing association, an~ as a teacher in
comprehensive schools and further education. Her
first novel, *Separate Tracks*, was published in 1983,
her second, *Her Living Image* (winner of the Somer-
set Maugham Award), in 1984, and her third, *The Ice
is Singing*, in 1987. She has also written a play for
Channel 4.

Since 1980 she has lived in Lancashire with her
two children, and combines writing with childcare
and occasional teaching of creative writing. She has
paid several extended visits to Australia, where her
family now live. In 1985–6 she was Arts Council
writer-in-residence at Northern College, Barnsley,
and in 1987–8, writing fellow at Sheffield Poly-
technic.

ff

JANE ROGERS

Separate Tracks

faber and faber

LONDON · BOSTON

First published in 1983
by Faber and Faber Limited
3 Queen Square London WC1N 3AU
This paperback edition first published in 1990

Printed in England by Clays Ltd, St Ives plc

© Jane Rogers, 1983

A CIP record for this book is
available from the British Library

ISBN 0–571–14100–5

2 4 6 8 10 9 7 5 3

FOR PEGGY AND ANDY

The sort of understanding I mean is inspired by love...

JOSEPH CONRAD, *The Mirror of the Sea*

PART ONE

Chapter 1

Daylight began to seep through the faded curtains. In the corner of the room a baby was crying. It made a thin, continuous bleating noise. A shape on the bed moved and a girl heaved herself up on one elbow. She remained still for a time, listening. At last she disentangled herself from the bed and crossed the room to the cot. She shook it viciously. The crying stopped. The girl stood still, staring down into the shadows in the cot. The room was cold, the light a matching harsh, watery grey. The backs of her skinny legs and arms glinted fish-belly white.

The crying began again. She lifted the baby, holding it over her shoulder and began to pace the room. The noise stopped but she continued to pace mechanically, patting the baby's back rhythmically as she walked. She was very young, her body still thin and gawky as an adolescent's but with something pinched about it. She had not been allowed to flesh out into maturity. In the relentless dawn light her head was more of a skull than a face, the dark hollowness of eye sockets intensified by the dull glaze of her eyes and the smeared black mascara around them. Thin white skin was stretched taut over cheek and jawbone. She walked with face raised, like someone blind.

The light brightened, exposing details in the squalid little room. A coat and jumper spread over the inadequate bedding. A soggy cardboard box full of dirty nappies. Maps of damp outlined on the faded wallpaper. When she stopped and laid him down, the baby began to cry again. She draped a coat around her shoulders and, taking a bottle from a cardboard box by the bed, left the room. In the bathroom she turned on the geyser and sat huddled on the edge of the bath. After an instant rush of cold water the geyser changed note, the flame suddenly leapt forwards then dwindled again, the tap spat, and a slow trickle of steaming hot water came out. She held the lower half of the bottle under the trickle, shaking it automatically so that a thin white froth formed on top of the liquid inside. When she took it to the baby, his open bleating mouth closed tight around the teat.

After she had fed him she dressed herself with slow automatic movements, and walked around the room, picking up items of clothing and putting them in a paper carrier bag. His renewed crying made a continuous sawing noise. When she had finished packing she examined her face in a small mirror which she took from her handbag. She looked at it impartially, as one might incuriously eye a stranger, and the expressionless white face looked back. She clicked the mirror shut, moving more quickly now. She placed a baby's bottle, a half-packet of powdered milk and a folded nappy on the bed. Two crumpled pieces of paper, extracted from her handbag, were carefully tucked under the powdered milk. She drew back the curtains. Then she picked up her carrier bag and went quickly out of the room, pulling the door to behind her. Incessant as drizzle, the weak bleating of the child continued in the empty room.

She notified the police that night, from a telephone box. The child was collected. The landlord gave her name and the information that she was four weeks behind with the rent. Children were not allowed. He had not known she had a baby. He did not know what she did for a living. The crumpled birth certificate told them that the baby

10

was Anthony John Childs, born 27 February 1963, father unknown.

Chapter 2

A family came on to the beach. They were running, panting with laughter, two adults swinging a child between them.

"One-and-two-and-three-and-*whee*!" Emma screamed and wriggled in her parents' grip, in an ecstasy of delight.

"And-two-and-three-and—whoops!" Richard stumbled and pretended to fall as they swung Emma up off the ground. The three of them collapsed in a heap on the sand.

"You little monster! YOU little horror—" on all fours, Richard thumped the sand behind Emma menacingly and she fled, squealing with laughter, looking back over her shoulder to make sure he was still chasing her.

Eileen picked up the duffle bag he had dropped and walked slowly after them. It was still early. There were only two groups of people on the beach. The tide was right out; the naked sand was rippled and dark with wet. Odd puddles of sea water flashed like mirrors in the sunlight. Richard caught up with Emma and scooped her up into the air, lifting her high and pretending to drop her. The child's screams echoed the shrieks of the seagulls drifting overhead. Richard set her down and she went trotting off on her unsteady toddler's legs over the sand, with a run that was nearly a stumbling fall at every step.

They spread towels on the dry sand above the tide line and went down to the water's edge. The lapping waves were no more than froth, so slight was the incline of the beach.

"Come on!" Richard went straight in, up to his knees. Emma stood on the edge laughing at him.

Eileen took her hand. "Come on. One at a time, look!" Raising her foot exaggeratedly high, as if going up a step, she stepped over the crest of the first little wave. Emma copied her, eyes suddenly widening as the cold water swirled about her feet. "See?" laughed Eileen, shivering. "It's nice, isn't it?"

"Come on," called Richard again, but Emma didn't want to go any further.

"You go on," Eileen told him, and led Emma along the edge of the sea, hopping over the shallow waves into the water and out on to the sand again. When they were tired of it they went up to lie on the towels.

Eileen scanned the bright water for Richard. At last she saw a black dot sliding up and down on the easy surface of the sea. She showed Emma how to dig through the dry crust to the damp sand underneath, and they scraped together a sandcastle out of it. He was a long time.

Suddenly his white torso reared up out of the water and he ran splashing up through the shallower waves. Eileen turned back to the sandcastle and concentrated on it.

"Look Emma, we'll put a door here." She could feel the sand vibrating as he ran up heavily behind her. At the last second she hurled herself sideways and he was stranded there, ludicrously shaking his wet hair like a dog over the space where she had sat.

"Not on the towel—not on the towel!" Eileen shrieked, immensely pleased with herself, fending him off. He flopped down on the towel, panting, flesh puckered by goosepimples.

"Look," commanded Emma. He raised his head and flopped down again like an old seal.

"Very nice."

12

"It's a castle."

"Uh huh."

"Emma, why don't you go and find some shells for it? See if you can find some nice shells or pebbles for windows and doors, OK?"

Emma stood up. "You come."

"In a minute, when Daddy's dry." Obediently Emma trotted off. Propped on one elbow, in the sudden intimacy of two, Eileen watched the drips on Richard's back move as he breathed. His back was broad, very white, with a few brown moles. On his shoulders the skin was speckled with pale freckles. She stroked one shoulder appraisingly. "I love your shoulders."

He spoke with his face resting sideways on the towel. "My shoulders? I can think of parts I'd rather have admired." He slid his hand between her thighs.

"It's cold," she objected.

"Never mind. It'll soon warm up." She lay down again, sideways facing him. The sun was getting stronger. She could begin to feel the warmth prickling her skin. They lay still, facing each other unsmilingly for a while. He began to move his hand gently up and down between her thighs.

"Look." Emma was back, with a fistful of shells.

"You need a big one," said Richard. "You need one of those big white ones for the door. Go and look over there." She ran off again.

"Pig," said Eileen, and moved closer to him. There was a delicious heat building up in them, from the sun, and each other.

Emma trotted off in the direction Richard had indicated until she came to the water's edge again. She picked up two black shells and followed the water line along. A lot more people had come on to the beach now. The sand was dotted with groups, clustered behind stripey windbreaks or beneath beach umbrellas. Each encampment was

13

made with a suitable respect for others' privacy, as if invisible lines divided them. A sprawl of possessions marked each territory—towels, clothes, lunch boxes, thermos flasks, sun-tan lotion. Newspapers and sunglasses protected people from visual contact within each group. The women mostly lay flat on the sand or in deck chairs, eyes closed against the sun, while the men sheltered behind the sports pages. Only children and dogs ignored the territorial lines and wandered noisily close to other groups. Some children ran down the beach in front of Emma and splashed straight into the water. She stood and stared at them, shells forgotten, watching the great sprays of water they kicked up.

Suddenly just behind her a large Alsatian bounded after them and into the sea. The speed and surprise of the animal bowled her over. Too shocked to cry, she scrambled up. Her sundress stuck wetly to her thighs. Wet sand was plastered to her bottom and legs. She looked at the crowds of people, waiting for attention— but no one on the beach had even noticed her. Then she started to run up the beach. But the wet sundress flapping against her legs made her even more unsteady than usual, and as she crossed over from hard wet sand to dry pitted sand she went sprawling again, face forwards. Sand went into her mouth and up her nose. She scrabbled up on to her knees and began to scream. Sand mixed with her saliva and slipped, gritty, to the back of her throat, making her choke till she was breathless. Quickly she worked herself up into a frenzy.

"Poor little mite."

"Wicked, isn't it?"

"Just listen to her, she's making herself ill, her mother should be shot."

Women poked their heads aggressively out of their nests. Emma regained her breath and gave full lung-power to her screams, penetrating all their carefully erected barriers. People shifted uneasily and glanced at

14

each other for reassurance. An angry-looking woman threw down her magazine and got up.

"I don't know," she said loudly to her husband. "Some people must have hearts of stone to listen to that poor child, they must really." She strode over to Emma and bent down, aware of her audience peering out from behind windbreaks and papers.

"What's the matter, love? Where's your Mummy, mmn?" Emma was lost, and the woman was strange; her screams rose to an even higher pitch, and her body went heavy and rigid when the woman tried to pick her up.

Eileen and Richard were rising like yeast in the sun. He brushed her ear with his lips.

"Let's go back to the hotel."

"Now?"

"Yes. We could put Emma down for a little nap."

Eileen giggled. "But we only just got up!" She wriggled round and laughed again. "You can't walk down the beach like that anyway."

"Don't see why not. Well, I'll put my trousers on if it offends you."

"It doesn't offend me." Her tone changed. "Richard, where's Emma?" She reared her head abruptly.

"Oh, she's around." Eileen didn't reply, scanning the beach for sight of the child. "She's around," he repeated. "She couldn't come to any harm with that sea. It's like a saucer of milk."

Eileen jumped up. "She's gone, Richard. Where is she?" She broke away at a run as he scrambled up.

"Eileen! Eileen!" But she continued to run awkwardly towards the sea. He pulled on his trousers and hurried after her. At the water's edge he hesitated, then turned to go along the beach in the opposite direction.

Eileen heard her before she saw her, a terrible sobbing shriek that rasped down the nerves of everyone within earshot.

"Mu-uh-uh-uuhh—" Three women stood near her, discussing what to do. She would not let any of them touch her. The terror in the sound clutched at Eileen, redoubling her fear before she could feel relief at seeing Emma in front of her. She ran and picked her up. The child's face was puffy and so besmeared with sand and snot that she was unrecognizable. Only slowly, very slowly, did the howls lessen, now punctuated by hiccups and sobs for breath. The three women who'd been trying to help turned away in disgust, muttering.

"Emma, Emma, ssh. Stop it. Hush, Mummy's here, it's all right."

"Mum-um-um- uh—" now a pathetic whimper.

Back at their camp Eileen hugged and rocked her, while Richard dabbed at the sandy swollen face with the corner of a towel.

"Silly girl, silly girl, sshh . . ." Eventually the sobbing gulps stopped. The little girl's face was strangely cleansed of expression.

"I wonder how she'll age?" Richard said suddenly.

"She looks like your mother," said Eileen.

"Yes, it's the puffiness around the eyes, I think."

"Poor baby, poor baby." Eileen clasped and rocked her, her own face still burning with shame. They were all three very sober for the afternoon, newly tender to one another. They went for a walk all the way along the beach, looking at the people, and in the rock pools for crabs.

16

Chapter 3

The long room hummed faintly; snores and snuffles of the babies were drowned by the business-like buzz of heating and ventilation machinery. Well-fitting blue blinds extinguished the outside world entirely. A red nightlight glowed on a table at one end of the room. In the carefully controlled darkness there were twelve wooden cots, each with a blue stick-on transfer of Dumbo the elephant at the head and each containing a baby lying on its right-hand side, tightly tucked in with a white cellular blanket.

Anthony John Childs lay in the cot at the end of the room furthest from the light. He was lying still, with his eyes open in the dark. One of the babies began to cry.

At 12.30 two night nurses came in with a tray of feeding bottles and picked up the first baby on the right and left side respectively. Most of the babies were whimpering now. Having tested the temperature of the milk by squirting a drop onto their wrists, the nurses began feeding. After they had fed each baby, they noted the volume of milk consumed on the child's feeding chart and changed the nappy, placing the dirty nappy in one of two bins labelled "damp" and "soiled". Then the baby was reinserted into its cellular envelope. When she had finished, the taller of the nurses went out and returned after a few minutes with two cups of coffee. Several of the babies were crying. The nurses sat and sipped their coffee.

"Beat you again."

"Where've you been tonight, then?" asked the smaller one.

"Just to the pub. I'm so bloody sleepy, I can't keep

my eyes open. Jeff gave me a lift again you know."

"He's getting fond."

"Huh. I expect he thinks I'll ask him in for a cup of coffee." She looked expressively round the room and burst into giggles.

"Sssh!" said the little one. "There's only one crying now."

"That new one." They both listened to the high angry cry. "He's got to learn," said the taller one philosophically, and took a sip of her coffee.

Four years later both nurses had left; but Anthony John Childs was still living in the children's home. The turnover of staff was high. They all looked much alike, in their pink checked uniforms, with their hair hygienically scraped back. When visitors came they were very nice, and on Sunday afternoons they got out the toy box and pushed dinky cars along the floor. Anthony John watched in silence, just as he watched Paul the new boy being hugged and wept over by his Mum, and Janice, beaming from ear to ear, leaving with her new Mum and Dad. On the television the Woodentop family bobbed through their adventures, and he watched with his blank incomprehending stare.

The matron at the home had high standards of cleanliness. In the evening the bath had to be scoured with Vim after each child's bath.

"Why d'ya do that?" asked a cheeky new lad, as the nurse bent and scrubbed, and Anthony John stood waiting in his dressing-gown.

"To kill all your—horrible—dirty—little—germs," hissed the nurse. She was stout, and had trouble reaching the area around the plughole.

At Christmas a man came from the Rotary Club, dressed up in a red coat and beard, and made some of the children cry. He gave each of them a brightly wrapped present. Anthony John's was a blue plastic boat, which

18

he kept in his pocket. It fell out when a young Irish nurse was undressing him for his bath, and she pounced on it.

"Isn't that nice now? I bet that'll float—shall we put it in the bath and see?" Clutching it in his hand, Anthony John was lifted into the bath, and the little boat was let loose. It bobbed up and down on the water, and the nurse swooshed her hand to make a wave. Anthony John watched, then tentatively poked at the boat with his finger. It ducked under the surface and bobbed up again. "See!" laughed the nurse.

An older woman came up behind her. "What on earth are you doing? She'll have a fit if she catches you with that." She reached down and grabbed the boat, and placed it at the back of the shelf that held the shampoo.

"What?"

The older woman knelt at her side by the bath. "No foreign objects in the bath. It's unhygienic, my dear—besides it's bathtime not playtime. Come on or you'll be out on your ear before you've even started. Have you washed him?"

The Irish girl shook her head and stood up, while the older woman heaved Anthony John to his feet and expertly lathered him. When his pyjamas had been put on he asked for his boat back.

"What? Oh yes, just a minute. Go and get in bed and I'll bring it for you. How many more are there, Kathleen? Jesus, you'll have to speed up a bit. Come on." The nurses usually speeded up around bathtime, because they could have a rest when everyone was in bed.

Next morning as he was cleaning his teeth Anthony John asked again for the boat, and got it. But the matron spotted it next to his plate at breakfast and asked whose it was.

"Mine."

"Where did you get it?"

"That man gave it me..."

"Which man?"

"With a red coat."

One of the nurses started to giggle. "He means Father Christmas."

"Oh well, this isn't the proper place for it, is it, Anthony John? When you have toys, they're for sharing with everybody, not for playing with at breakfast time." She picked up the boat and put it in her pocket.

"But—"

"Don't answer back, Anthony John. It's cheeky. We'll put it in the toy box with the other toys so that everybody can play with it."

That afternoon she did slip it into the toy box, and Anthony John sat near the toy box and guarded it—but just the same, two days later, it vanished.

Anthony John Childs was not a favourite with the nurses. He was not quick or funny, and he had a pale sulky face. Worse than that, he wet his bed, long after he should have stopped.

"Come on, stinky," said the nurse as he queued up to be dressed in the morning. "God, nobody'd believe you had a bath last night. Yeuch!" They argued over who would make his bed, because the sheets always needed changing, and the beds were heavy and had to be pulled right out from the wall.

The nurses used to take the children out to the park on nice afternoons, in threes, a pushchair and one child holding on to each side. In the summer when Anthony John was three, there was a new nurse called Winnie. Sometimes in the park Winnie would let one of the children push the pushchair, or she would push with one hand and hold hands with the other. Her hands were plump and sweaty. Anthony John liked to hold hands with her. She left in September though, because she was pregnant. The matron confided to her deputy that it was just as well really. Winnie would never have made a good nursery nurse, she was too affectionate with them. And she had favourites. "It's not fair to the children—and we're left with tears when she swans off."

Anthony John did not cry.

At six years he was moved into a family group home, where seven other children, all older than himself, lived with a housemother and assistant. He displayed no emotions whatsoever at the move, and according to his social worker's case notes, he settled in well in his new home. He continued to wet the bed, however.

At school he made a slow start. The teacher listened to him reading for ten minutes each day.

"'Here we are at home,' says Daddy. Peter helps Daddy with the car, and Jane helps Mummy get the tea. 'Good girl,' says Mummy to Jane. 'You are a good girl to help me like this.'"

His blank expression, air of passivity and scrupulously clean clothes helped the teacher to pinpoint his background and abilities very quickly. She encouraged him to join in group games and remembered to say "or any grown-up you know" when she asked the class to draw pictures of Mummy and Daddy. But Anthony John's drawings were never particularly recognizable. He seemed rather backward.

When he was seven he had his first fight. They had been told to line up in twos in the playground to walk down to church for Harvest Festival. Most of them were carrying things—vegetables, flowers, tins of peaches. Anthony was paired with Amelia, another class outcast, who had been sent home in disgrace one day for coming to school without any knickers.

"Hold hands!" called out the teacher when they came to cross the road, and Anthony obediently took Amelia's hand. When they reached the other side of the road, he was pushed from behind.

"Cissy! Cissy! Holding hands with a girl!" Craig Fisher was holding a Saran-wrap covered fruit bowl full of

21

carefully arranged oranges and bananas, and he prodded
Anthony with it viciously in the small of the back.
Anthony let go Amelia's hand and turned round,
presenting his chest to Craig's attacks and staring
stupidly. Only after four or five further blows did he
raise his right arm and, with a slightly surprised
expression, knock the fruit bowl flying.

Anthony fought badly—it was the first time he had
ever done it—but he was heavy for his age and the other
boy was not expecting him to retaliate. They ended up
rolling on the ground and Anthony did not loose his grip
until the teacher pulled them apart. Craig's nose was
bleeding and he was crying noisily. The teacher wiped
him with a tissue. Afterwards several people, including
Anthony himself, admitted that he had hit Craig first
and spoilt his lovely bowl of fruit.

"Why?" demanded the headmaster.

"He called me a cissy."

"Well," said the headmaster, "well, what a silly boy
you are. Haven't you ever heard the old saying 'Sticks
and stones may break my bones but words will never
hurt me'? Why did he call you a cissy?"

Anthony would not say at first. Eventually he
muttered, "Holding hands."

"For holding hands?"

"With Amelia."

The headmaster stared at him reflectively. He would
ask Mrs Francis not to make girls and boys hold hands in
a crocodile, he decided. They were quite capable of
walking on their own.

"Well, he's a silly boy, but that doesn't mean you can
go and hit him. I'm going to make you stay in every
lunchtime this week so that you understand that you
must not fight. NEVER take the law into your own
hands. Do you understand, Anthony?"

Staying in for a week was pleasant for Anthony. He
acquired a certain status in the other children's eyes, for

the first time in his life. And Mrs Francis sat at her desk
and marked books, and gave him a Polo now and again,
and the classroom was quiet and peaceful.

He got a reputation for fighting, and parents told their
children to keep away from him. When he left primary
school he was known as the school bully, heavy and pasty
and feared.

Chapter 4

Emma remembered the times when she was hit as a
child. In particular she remembered being hit by her
mother for walking on the kitchen floor. When she was
five she had come in from playing one hot day, breathless
and excited, her friends waiting outside. She needed to
go to the toilet. Eileen was scrubbing the kitchen floor.
She worked vigorously, kneeling on a folded-up piece of
old curtain, putting the whole weight of her body into the
scrubbing of the red earthenware flags. She was panting
with effort, and Emma saw with dismay that the way
through to upstairs was gleaming wet and puddled. She
knew she wasn't allowed to walk on the wet floor—it
made footprints. She stood in the doorway with her legs
crossed. Eileen's back was to her, head bent down over
the scrubbing brush, jerking back and forth furiously
with each scrub. Emma was always aware of that as
something peculiar to her mother. She cleaned her teeth
with the same sort of furious frenzy, shaking her whole
body. No one else did it like that.

"Mummy?" Eileen didn't hear her. "Mummy!"

Her mother put the brush in the bucket and sat back
on her heels. "What?" Not looking round.

"Mummy, can I go to the toilet?"

Her mother sighed. "Yes, go on. Take big steps."

Exaggeratedly, on tip-toe, Emma stepped across the wet floor, and looked back from the door to see the footprints slowly filling with water again. Like a sponge. Her weight squeezed out the water for a minute.

She ran upstairs, weed so quickly that there was still a little dribble coming out as she pulled up her pants and rushed down again. They were going to play at show-jumping over the clothes prop. She flung open the door and started the giant steps over the kitchen floor, staring down at her feet. Her mother, kneeling over her brush, suddenly coiled and lashed at her—a stinging slap on the leg. Emma nearly lost her balance, staggered and stood stock still. Tears sprang to her eyes automatically.

"Look!" her mother shouted, pointing at the footprints. "Get out—go on, get out!"

Emma began to howl with pain and hobbled to the doorway clutching her leg. "I asked you!" she cried. "I wanted to wee, you said I could go—" She was overwhelmed by the unfairness of the slap.

Eileen threw down her brush and stood up, and Emma was shocked into silence. Her mother's face was terrible, not looking at her. "I don't care," she said. Her voice was low and harsh. "That's my lot, isn't it. Down on my knees while you traipse in and out—a living bloody doormat!" Her face was contorted, her eyes found Emma and stared at her. "I've had it. I'm sick of it. SICK of you!" And her face crumpled horribly into crying and she blundered out of the room, upstairs.

Emma stood there in terror looking at the floor and the footprints. Mummy was crying. She didn't know what to do. She didn't dare walk across the floor again. She could hear her mother's harsh awful sobbing from upstairs. It was her fault but what had she done? Her leg was bright red where the wet hand had slapped it. What now? She had never heard her mother crying before—she had never imagined she did, or could. And what for? No one had hurt her. Just because Emma had walked on the wet

24

floor? She knew it couldn't be, and the inability to understand made her almost frantic. "I'm sick of you." Would she run away? Emma was desperate to make it all right again. She walked gingerly across the floor and, taking the piece of curtain in both hands, crawled backwards across the floor rubbing out all the footprints. It left a smeary dry pathway across the middle of the room. The noise was still coming from upstairs. She didn't know what to do. She went upstairs. Frightened into crying again herself now, she opened the bedroom door.

"Mummy? Mummy?"

Her mother's red swollen face lurched up from the pillow. Her voice was soft and funny. "It's all right, Emma. Go and play, I'll be all right in a minute."

Crying thick and fast now, in panic. "Mummy, Mummy!"

The puffy face smiled strangely. "I'm all right, Emma. I'm coming in a minute. We'll go and buy some sweets, all right? You go downstairs, I'll come in a minute."

"I wiped the floor," sobbed the child.

Her mother gave a strangled laugh. "It's not the floor," she said. "That's the least of my worries."

Emma quieted, but with a coldness in her. It wasn't the floor—it wasn't her. She and her mother were in separate worlds.

Once her father had gone away somewhere, she didn't know where. It was just before Easter. Her mother had gone peculiar, very gentle spoken and kind where usually she was sharp. Emma understood enough to know that something was wrong and her mother unhappy, and she tried desperately to please her. She laid tables and washed up and made beds, and her mother seemed to notice nothing, always the same, that awful gentle smile and far-away-seeing eyes, as if her life had turned to slow motion. At school they were

25

making Easter cards and Emma stayed in at morning and afternoon break to work on hers. It was a deep blue card with a crêpe paper daffodil, finely shredded yellow petals stuck on over and over each other so that her flower blossomed and glowed out of the dark background. It was really beautiful. Inside, Emma wrote in her round neat handwriting, "Happy Easter to Mummy, lots of love from Emma x x x".

On Easter morning she put it in front of her mother's plate at breakfast, and Eileen picked it up and glanced at it. "That's pretty, Emma. Why haven't you put it to Daddy?"

"He's not here."

"That's very unkind. He's sent you some Easter eggs, hasn't he? He'll be very upset."

"It's for you," said the little girl fiercely.

"I don't want a card just for me." And she put the card down again and didn't say anything else about it. She didn't even look at the separate orange and yellow petals of the daffodil that had been stuck over each other, each with a tiny separate blob of glue, thirty of them.

Chapter 5

Emma was an intelligent child and did extremely well at school. Both Eileen and Richard were excited by her progress and did all they could to encourage her. By the time she was ten she was reading omnivorously; books, comics, magazines—everything from Dickens to the *Dandy*.

Whenever she visited her Aunty she brought back a pile of magazines with her. She didn't admit to herself that she was hiding them from Eileen, but somehow they were always at the bottom of her satchel and didn't see the light until she was safely shut in her bedroom. *Woman, Woman's Own, Woman's Realm*, crammed with helpful home-making hints, holiday fashions and prize-winning recipes. Her glazed mind skimmed over this wealth, in greedy search of FICTION. "Fiction" was usually written in elegant curly script, and often the promised page was lusciously coloured in midnight blue, deep purples or reds. Girls with exquisite profiles stood on lonely promontories with their long fair or glossy dark hair windswept around their shoulders. She read as a connoisseur, in delicious anticipation of the next move.

At the gate he looked back, to see her as he would always remember her, frail, beautiful, one arm outstretched towards him... "It's no good, Malcolm," she gulped, bravely holding the tears back. "I can never marry you. I made a promise." Suddenly his strong hands were grasping her shoulders, and the two brightest, funniest, most serious eyes in the world were gazing deeply into her own.

She read them gluttonously, as if she had a box of chocolates she was determined not to share. Often she stayed awake till one or two in the morning, her bed littered with consumed magazines. It was as if her appetite for romance could never be satisfied. But when she set off for school in the mornings they were stowed neatly out of sight under her bed. Reading them was always accompanied by a frisson of guilt.

One day when she came home from school they were in two big piles on the kitchen table.

"Are those yours?" said Eileen.

"No, I just borrowed them from Aunty May."

"Oh," said Eileen brightly. "I was having a tidy-out. You don't want to keep that sort of drivel do you?"

The girl was humiliated and angry. She knew perfectly well that Eileen did not tidy out her room, but had been snooping around there, and that she despised

27

that type of magazine. She always scoffed about the women who read them at the hairdresser's. "What slop!"

They were thrown away and Emma didn't take magazines home any more, but read them greedily and surreptitiously at her aunt's, while her aunt watched telly and talked to the newsreaders.

Chapter 6

Richard left Eileen when Emma was ten and a half, and came back a year later. Emma was glad he had come back. When she was fourteen he left again. He didn't want to lose touch with his daughter, and arranged to see her every month or so. Gradually these visits grew more sporadic, and Richard came to dread them.

Emma looked forward to them inordinately, then found herself sullen and tongue-tied in her father's presence. She wasn't what he wanted her to be, she knew. She owed it to her abandoned mother to show disapproval and to not have a good time. She wanted him to like her and she was sure he didn't. Her mother said often enough, "He's seeing you out of duty, you know." The only retaliation left to the girl, then, was to show even less enthusiasm than he.

In the summer of her fifteenth birthday he was working in Liverpool and invited her there for the day because he had not seen her since Easter. He went to Lime Street Station to meet her. Standing at the ticket barrier, he stared intently at the people spilling out of the train, searching her out. He wondered what she would be wearing. For no obvious reason his eyes kept returning to a figure moving slowly along the outside of the platform. Dutifully he turned back to scan the oncoming crowd, hoping to recognize her. Only when she was a few feet away did he realize that she had been that slow-moving figure. He wanted to laugh at himself for his lack of faith. Like a city boy who is shown the leaves and flowers of a potato plant and told to dig up the vegetable roots, stupidly amazed by the discovery of the predicted golden fruits in the earth.

He smiled broadly at her, and she gave an embarrassed little nod, colouring as she handed her ticket to the collector.

"It's a return." Richard hugged her, and felt her squirm with embarrassment as he did so.

She released herself quickly, fumbling with her bag and her ticket. "Which way out?"

He led the way, glancing sideways at her face, which was composed into a careful mask. The station was crowded and oppressively hot, and outside was much the same. The sky above the city was a grey lid, the air that lay under it stale and overused. Richard took her into a coffeeshop. They sat in silence till the waitress had brought their drinks.

'Well, how are you then? You're looking extremely demure."

"Demure?" Irritation flickered in her face.

"Yes, demure; self-contained, ladylike, prim and proper."

"Huh." She picked up her coffee spoon and started drawing tentacles out of a few drips of spilt coffee on the formica table. Richard saw himself unpleasantly clearly, as an ageing stranger with nothing to say, trying to jolly a reaction out of her. Don't ask about Eileen. Or school, yet—wearily he cast about among the prickly subjects for a way in to communication.

"Nice journey?"

"OK."

'When did you break up?"

"July 18th."

"And have you any great plans for the summer?"

She shook her head. "I might go cycling with Chris."

Christine. A stupid horsey girl. "That will be nice... Whereabouts?"

"Dunno, maybe in Cornwall."

"It'll be crowded down there this time of year. You might be better off in East Anglia... it's nice and flat there."

"But there's nothing to see."

He stopped himself from asking how she knew that since she'd never been, and asked her what she'd like to do today. She shrugged, as he had known she would. He outlined his carefully laid plans-for-a-daughter-who-is-determined-to-be-bored. A visit to the African collection in the museum (last time they met, she had told him about a TV programme on the Masai that she had been interested by; probably she'd forgotten). A pub lunch and then delicious rest, a film matinee of her choice. From there it was downhill all the way—maybe a stroll by the river, a nice meal—and he could pack her off on the nine-thirty train. She listened without changing expression, in silence.

"Well, let's be off, shall we?" He tried to subdue the anger in his voice. "I wouldn't like you to get bored."

They went down to the museum. Under the oppressive grey sky, a slight heat haze shimmered. Richard's eyes pricked in the glare, as if grains of sand had been sprinkled in them. He blinked, imagining that his eyelids could stick to his eyeballs. Crossing a busy road he unthinkingly reached for Emma's hand. Safe on the other side, he was surprised by it. She did not let go, though his own hand was sticky with sweat, and he did not dare to release her, afraid of seeming to reject this passive advance.

At the museum she betrayed no recollection of her interest in the Masai, but obediently followed him around the exotic masks and fetishes, stopping and staring when he pointed to an item of interest. The

30

colour and vigour of the ancient faces gave him, as always, a surge of pleasure, recharging him with energy. She was quite untouched. As he turned from the furious passion of the masks to his expressionless child, he felt himself becoming desperate. Surely there was a response in her somewhere?

"Look at this one—my favourite!" The case contained a carved warrior, big as a ten-year-old child, grimacing through the glass with fixed, crossed eyes. Beneath his flat wooden belly proudly rose the remains of what must have been a gigantic penis. It had been rudely sliced off at a length of three inches or so—to placate a missionary, Richard assumed.

"Isn't he fine? A real victim of Christianity—cut short in his prime!"

The girl flushed to the roots of her hair and moved away abruptly. Her embarrassment was electric. He wondered if he had done it deliberately. What was subconsciously at work now? Perhaps he was merely playing the role she expected of him—crude, insensitive. He was aware of a certain pleasure at having embarrassed her. He had found a nerve he could touch, even though it would make her bury herself more deeply.

Emma moved on to the Egyptian section and with infuriating slowness paused to examine each pot, each fragment of stone and dusty utensil on display. He stared unseeingly through the window, willing the day to end. There would be a terrible fuss if he sent her home now though;

"You deign to see her for one day after three whole months, and then you send her packing at lunchtime..." He could hear Eileen's indignant telephone crescendo.

And himself; "There's no point in my seeing her. She's yours." A nauseating wave of self-pity swept him to gather her up and take her to lunch. At least he could have a drink.

He refrained from drawing her attention to the mosaic

round the bar and the idiosyncratic carvings. Who in their right mind could expect the girl to be interested? He wondered if she had any interests, now. He downed a couple of pints as she sipped her half of shandy. She had told him she didn't go to pubs.

"What do you do with yourself of an evening, if you don't go to pubs?"

Her hands twitched on the table top. He felt a distant pity. "I read. Sometimes I go out. The bus service isn't very good."

He stared at the bar and with a slow refocusing saw the pot-bellied men standing there and the dry curls of blue smoke in the air, the weight of brown panelling and the unhappy stranger tacked to the table beside him with a sticky glass. He wouldn't ask to see her again.

He rose and she followed him out. He walked at his normal speed, she had to do little runs to keep up.

"Why are you in such a hurry?" she asked.

"It's not a very pleasant walk," he replied savagely.

"D'you like that dress?" A long haired girl in a billowing Indian dress passed them on the other side of the road. It was deep blue with red and gold patterns on it.

He considered. "Yes. It's a bit like wearing a label though, isn't it? You can bet she burns joss sticks and was a flower child and eats vegetarian food." Too late he asked, "Do you like it?"

"Yes," she said. "Well, to look at. I don't suppose I'd wear one."

He was sorry for his clumsiness. "What sort of clothes do you like?" He would soon be out of his depth.

"Oh, it depends." She sounded almost eager. "I love some, you know, that I could never wear—really slinky things, crêpe and sequins..."

"Why could you never wear them?"

"Well, where would I?" There was no answer. The speed of their walking had made him sweat all over and his shirt was sticking to him. Mingled with the stale petrol smells of the street, he could scent his own bitter sweat.

She had chosen *Gone with the Wind*. Though the cinema was like the inside of an oven, he lay back in his seat with thankfulness and let the lurid colours and emotions of the film lap over him.

At the end she said, "It was good, wasn't it?" She had enjoyed something today at least then. "Are we going to the river now?"

He glanced at her. "Well, how tired are you? It's a fair walk."

"That's OK. I'd like to see the sea."

He was unpleasantly surprised. "But you can't see the sea from here. It's just a river—an estuary—you know, like the Thames."

"How far down does the sea begin?"

"Well, it's hard to say—the tide comes up, I mean it's sea after a bit, you couldn't actually say it begins or ends here. . ."

"Ah." She was staring at her feet. She seemed disappointed, though he couldn't see why.

"What's so special about the sea?"

"Dunno. I just fancied it. It's hot, isn't it?"

"Yes, do you think it will rain?"

"I hope there'll be a storm!" she said, almost enthusiastically.

From the immense depths of his weariness he tried to summon up a little kindness. She was obviously coming out of her shell a bit, even if he no longer could. Give the girl a chance. "OK. Let's go. We'll walk to the ferry."

"Good."

The awful silence came down on them again, and he dared with the question he'd been biting back all day. "How's your mother?"

"All right." The silence continued. Fair enough. Fair enough. He told himself he had no right to

33

expect more. They started to go downhill.

The girl stopped suddenly. "Can you smell it?"

"What?"

She sniffed exaggeratedly. "The sea! You can smell it!" She quickened her pace. He could smell nothing. But he caught a glint of moving water between the rooftops and pointed it out to her.

"I can see," she said irritably, as if she had had it in view for hours. As they went down the hill, the water appeared as a backdrop to every building, in fluid motion behind the solid ranks of stone. The girl ran the last hundred yards or so and on to the wooden jetty for the ferries. She went as close as she could get to the water, hanging over the rail. He caught her up. Her face had come to life.

"It's lovely! Smell it! It smells of the sea—and it's so wide—it's lovely!" Inadequate before her enthusiasm, he looked across the grey slopping waters.

"Look!" She pointed down river, where the dirty waters were flanked with grey smoking chimneys, warehouses and a distant red barge.

He didn't know what to say. Guide-book talk to the rescue. "That's Birkenhead on the other side. You can cross by ferry."

She looked across. "There aren't any bridges."

"No," he said. "There's the tunnel."

"Yes, but there aren't any bridges are there?" she said insistently.

"No."

"I hate tunnels. I wouldn't go under there for anything. Never. Dark, and shut in, when you could be—" She stared around her again, her eyes alight.

He felt the need of some answering gesture to this exuberance. "Would you like to go on the ferry?"

She hesitated. "Can we?"

"Of course we can. It only takes ten minutes."

"Oh, can we? I'd love to."

34

The bell rang as they stepped on, they were nearly the last. She rushed up to the front of the boat and positioned herself like a figurehead, face to the wind. The boat swung round and started to move across the water. He sat next to his daughter, watching her.

"Look," she commanded. "The water, it just goes on— oh! it smells of going away, of holidays—" He looked down the river, his eyes following the thick ribbon of water through the city, and saw its fluid silver beauty and at the same instant felt the hesitancy of the deck under his feet rising to meet a wave. He was afloat, with the lit moving sea before him.

"I wish it wouldn't land," she said passionately, staring towards the sea. And so do I. Sudden love lashed against him and he stretched his hand blindly to grasp her warm shoulder. The dry day washed away, and silver water rippled and shone on all sides.

Looking back on that day, the girl always experienced the uncleanness of guilt, though she had not exactly lied.

It had been a boring day. What was the use? He'd taken her to his usual old buildings and museums and lectured her for hours and tried to ask her things and make her feel ignorant. And despised her for wanting to see *Gone with the Wind*. Finally, they'd gone to the river. That cheered her up, but he seemed to be—he'd stopped being superior and gone all soppy. What other word was there for it? Till she had actually felt superior, as if he was in her power in some way. She skirted and avoided the incident in her memory as she would have avoided repeating a dirty joke.

It was the last time, really, that he would have any effect on her. That day stayed hot in her memory in a way that later encounters did not. They did not understand each other. She felt she was able to discard him painlessly—part of the past, of when she was little and didn't understand. From now on she would

35

understand. She would be on equal terms with people. The world was full of more interesting people, who were not so difficult and embarrassing.

Looking back on that day, her father remembered the way the water had lifted the boards that they stood on. He remembered a poignant moment of closeness with his daughter; an oasis. He determined to try to see his daughter more often and cultivate the closeness which, despite all his mistakes, existed between them.

Chapter 7

Eileen waited up for Emma after her visit to her father. Eileen had been a nervous child, often subject to butterflies in the tummy. Today her stomach had been churning continuously. When she went to the toilet, the food she had eaten shot out of her in a scalding watery brown jet. She knew why. Him. She certainly didn't think he would ever come back. But the walls of her stomach seemed to know differently.

By late evening she is sitting straight-backed at the dining table, controlling her breathing. She makes herself the image of a coal fire, where she must labour to keep the heat fierce and to rake out from the glowing face of the fire any sticks or coals or individual items so that only the red heat of the pain is there and she's not distracted by incidents. She must hold in her head the red pain he has made, and not be betrayed by the watery longings of a weak stomach.

She sits with her feet flat on the floor, hollow back not supported by the chair. Hair black streaked with silver, shoulder length, untidy. Face wrinkled but not old; her skin is of the softness that melts to touch (as he had often quoted to her), flesh the senses dip into at each brushing

36

contact. But softness can be revolting too, making you recoil as if you've touched something forbidden—almost as if the skin had been peeled off and you touch the awful silken bloody softness of the naked flesh inside. She rarely kissed Emma, but she had done so that morning and Emma's own skin had crawled at the contact of that too-soft cheek; she had been appalled by the death in her mother's skin.

The softness on her face is puffy now (though the face itself is strong, high cheekbones, determined mouth). The eyes are tightly closed, the face tilted slightly upwards. She is breathing firmly and regularly, as if in preparation for swimming underwater. If her concentration is shifted for a second, her lungs will leap out like crazy frogs, her head and feet will spin off, she will explode like a worn-out star. Footsteps on the path. One set. The sound of Emma trying to open the door. Still her body is rigid, she knows, she has *heard* that he isn't here—but her stomach doesn't yet. Rustle of Emma hanging up her coat. Footsteps of Emma walking to the kitchen. Definitely, only Emma.

She sits back slowly, untying the knots in her muscles. Is guilty at being discovered sitting idle and hurries towards the kitchen. Emma is looking in the fridge and is surprised to see her mother. She expected her to be in bed.

Eileen sits at the kitchen table. "There's some pressed beef on the bottom shelf. Are you hungry?"

"I shouldn't be, we had a three course meal. But it seems a long time ago." Emma gets out the beef and tomatoes and finds a knife. Her mother watches her. She's very pretty, very self-possessed. Does she look like me? She looks more knowing. But did Richard think so?

The silence is too long. "Want some?" asks Emma, indicating the beef with her knife.

Eileen shakes her head. "Did you have a nice time?" Emma's mouth is full, she chews ostentatiously. The two

37

women are alone in the world in the fluorescent bright kitchen with the black sky leaning against the window.

Emma swallows. "OK. We went to a museum, the cinema, and on a ferry."

"You were out all day then?"

Emma nodded. "We went to a pub at lunchtime." Eileen wouldn't let her go to pubs.

"Well, was it fun?"

"It wasn't special. The ferry was nice." She filled her mouth with half a tomato and chewed stolidly.

Eileen stared at the table top. Her stomach was quietening. She would be hungry soon. "Well, what did he have to say?"

Emma frowned. "Not much. I always feel as if he's expecting me to say things. He doesn't talk about anything." Eileen was glad. She was jealous. "He showed me this disgusting object in the museum." Emma regretted that as soon as she'd said it.

"Well—what?"

"An African-type thing."

"Yes?"

"Like a statue, without any clothes on. A man."

"Oh, really?"

"Not very realistic—an effigy type of thing."

"Ah. Well, what was so disgusting about it?" Her father's words about the statue being "cut off" still rang in Emma's ears, it struck her as deeply obscene. She was embarrassed.

Eileen was more and more intent. "Go on!"

There was no way out. "Dad just said—well, it had been broken—*you* know—and Dad said he'd been cut off."

"He?"

"The statue."

Eileen stared at her. She was repelled by the thought of them mentioning anything sexual. She imagined now how close they had stood, that Richard had perhaps kissed Emma when she arrived, how he had looked at her. He'd taken her to a pub. She was an adult in his eyes. Her stomach sides convulsed towards each other again. "So what did you say?" Her eyes were staring madly.

"I didn't say anything." Emma felt ashamed and frightened.

Eileen walked over and stared at the black outside. She would never know. "How's his lady friend?"

Emma sounded relieved. "I don't know, Mum. We didn't talk about her."

Eileen took the cigarettes from her pocket and lit one. She exhaled slowly. She wished she could blow him out like that. The helpful tone in Emma's voice just now grated on her; what had she got to hide? Why shouldn't she say what they'd talked about all day? He was her husband, wasn't he?

Forcing herself to be patient she sat down again. Emma's watching face irritated her. The sound of Emma chewing was maddening. "Well?"

"Well what?"

"Is that all there is to say?"

"I've told you Mum, it was boring. We just walked round these places all day." Injured irritation was audible in Emma's voice. It rose in pitch. "I'm sorry I didn't take a tape recording for you. All right, in the museum: 'Notice the detail on that nineteenth-century Ashanti mask, wonderful craftsmanship don't you think? Pay particular attention to the medieval curlicues—'" Her face was red, she put on an imitation of her father's very correct accent, and her voice got louder.

Eileen suddenly leaned across the table and swiped at her, hitting the side of her head.

"What's that for?" Holding her cheek.

"He's your father. You don't care a damn for anyone, do you? He's taken you out, tried to talk to you and interest you and all you can do—" She stopped. She

39

didn't mean that. She could hear her own voice, she wanted to hit Emma, she wanted him not to have wasted his time with the silly little bitch, and she wanted her husband and daughter to have had a good time and loved each other like a father and child should, and she was glad they hadn't. Why should he be happy and understood, why should he expect to swan into their daughter's life and be loved? But his face ... his eyes in Emma's now. She could hear his voice in the poor parody, know keenly that hesitant, pompous politeness that is one of his defences. See his arm half-outstretched around the shoulder to shepherd you to the next picture, looking at your face to see if you like it, his voice moving from politeness into nearness.

Staring at the table top, she can hear Emma snivelling. She looks up and what can you say to the girl it's not her fault. "I'm sorry." She knows Emma senses a weakness and will play it.

"Well, I don't see what it's for. You can't just go round slapping people for no reason. Unless you're mad."

Exaggerated patience, Eileen leans forward arms folded on the table top. "I hit you because I was angry. I'm sorry because I wasn't really angry with you. I was angry at your father."

Emma rose, triumphant. "Well, bloody well go and hit him. I'm sick of getting it from both of you." She flung out of the door and, fish on the line, Eileen was tugged to her feet.

"What do you mean from both of us? What did he do?"

Emma locked herself in the bathroom and shouted through the door, "Go and ask him yourself. It's not my mess, it's yours. I'm not your messenger—I've got my own life to live." She turned the tap on, wincing at her own melodrama.

Eileen, leaning against the kitchen doorpost, detected the falseness in her daughter's tone but was philosophical now. Why shouldn't she act? And the part they gave her certainly wasn't fair, since they got all the histrionics and the poor child had to play continuity between them. She went slowly to lock the front and back doors and put the food away in the fridge. The silence, and odd noises in it, were loud in her ears. The fridge hummed for a minute when she closed the door. Water from the bathroom ran down the drain outside. A car passed, Emma's footsteps went quickly from the bathroom to her bedroom, the door shut. Silence.

Eileen watched her own reflection in the black window above the sink. She was a woman in a kitchen. She looked perfectly complete and normal. Each object in the kitchen stood out in the stillness with an identity of its own, teapot, herb jars, yellow Sunlight washing-up liquid. And there was she, hugging herself, staring out of the middle of it. In her house, in her life. It was all right. She walked to the door on tiptoe to not disturb it, turned off the light silently and went to bed comforted, like an open-mouthed child given the dummy.

Chapter 8

When he started secondary school, Anthony became an instant target for second and third years. He was unpopular with other first years, and so could often be found alone and vulnerable to attack. The teachers were quick to recognize him as a tale-teller; his persecutors were rarely punished. Besides, he was ugly and stupid, and thoroughly deserved it.

Five weeks after the beginning of term, he was picked up by police at 11 o'clock on a Wednesday morning. He was standing outside a television rental shop, staring at the test card on the screen in the window. They took him back to school, where he was caned. The headmaster asked him the reason for his truancy and as a result a special assembly was held the next morning, at which they were all warned of heavy punishments in store for bullies. After a few days things reverted to normal and, having discovered that no one minded as long as you didn't get caught, Anthony continued to play truant two or three days a fortnight. When the reason for his absence filtered down to his form teacher, though, his teacher made time for a little talk with Anthony. He was sorry for the lad—what a start in life! But he didn't think this tale-telling and punishing of bullies was the answer at all.

"You've got to learn to stick up for yourself, lad. That way, they won't always be after you, you see? If you can defend yourself, well, you're laughing aren't you? Why don't you go along to Mr Clay's junior boxing club on Thursday after school and pick up a few tips, eh?"

Having been reminded again on Thursday, Anthony went to the boxing club, which had only three first year recruits, and where he was consequently welcomed. And throughout the course of his school career he attended boxing club sporadically and became a competent boxer, by the school's standards. His teachers seized on the fact with relief when he got to the fifth year and it was time for reports and careers references: boxing was the only hobby or interest they could find.

Chapter 9

Emma met Anthony when she took a temporary job at the family group home where he was raised. The address was a number on Prospect Crescent. She got lost trying to find it. The bus dropped her on what seemed to be a country lane, bordered to the left by fields. She turned off right, into Hope Street. Hope Street formed a T-junction with Independence Avenue. The far end of Independence Avenue was a cul de sac, but Sunrise Avenue and Bright Street formed junctions with it. Promise Crescent and Dawn Crescent led off Sunrise Avenue but they were both cul-de-sacs. Sunrise Avenue met Bright Street again at the end.

Emma was in new country. The peculiar layout of the streets, the absence of traffic and the remarkable similarity of all the houses contributed to the sense of foreignness. She had never walked anywhere before where the streets were not arranged in blocks. She had never walked through a council estate. She went up Bright Street and came out at Independence Avenue again. She wasn't sure if she'd been there before. The houses were grey pebble dash, their doors were green. Half-net curtains bandaged the windows. In front of each semi-detached pair of houses lay a rectangle of yellowish grass circumscribed by a narrow concrete footpath. There was no one in sight.

53 Prospect Crescent was just like the others. When the door opened, there was a smiling, pink-clad woman and a doll on a chair. "Hello, love."

"Mrs Garter?"

"That's me, love—you *have* made good time—I didn't think you'd be here before tea—I'm ever so pleased to see you I've been on my own for three and a half weeks now since the last one left—three and a half weeks—they don't give a damn up at county hall they just leave you to rot—come on—" She seemed to speak without breathing. Emma looked up the stairs and saw two small black faces watching her through the banisters. She smiled awkwardly, but the children maintained fixed stares.

"The cleaner comes in, of course, but it's not the same, it's the responsibility that gets you—cleaning's the easy part of it d'you like housework? You do look young my dear, how old are you? You can't be much older than

43

some of the children—don't you worry about them they're all right when you get to know them you won't have any trouble you'll be one of the family in a day or two—" She led the way to the kitchen.

Mrs Garter was fat and smelled of disinfectant. The outlines of her dark-coloured lacy slip were visible through her pink nylon housecoat. In the kitchen she started telling the histories of the children in a loud, confidential tone. Emma was embarrassed by her intimacy; she sat on the edge of a kitchen chair with her eyes averted from the woman's fleshy friendly face. She stared at the walls, at the eight hooks with matching mugs, the eight pairs of wellies lined up by the door, the eight named coat-hooks. She strained her ears for any sound of children, but there was nothing. The woman's voice demanded attention, laced with the headline language of violence and scandal. "Ever such a nice woman" had kept the little girl called Delia locked in a bedroom in her own filth for six months, only shoving a bowl of food through the door from time to time. She'd taken against Delia, apparently, though she had four others whom she looked after beautifully. "Mind you, they've all got different fathers!" said Mrs Garter. "They're all the colours of the rainbow!"

Mrs Garter took her round the house, and Emma received a fleeting impression of small clean rooms with bunk beds and labelled drawers. Mrs Garter's own room was in a different style, florid and fussy. Every item of furniture seemed to be wearing a frilly pink skirt.

Delia was jet black. Emma recognized one of the faces that had stared through the banisters. Delia only seemed to know how to stare. Mrs Garter talked on in the child's hearing. Delia had come on well, she wasn't half so wild. She couldn't even feed herself when she came. Wicked, wasn't it? Delia's white eyes followed the movements of Mrs Garter's thick wrist hoisting the teapot. The other children stared at

44

their plates. They weren't allowed to talk at meals.

The table was set with a dish of red jam at each end and a fluorescent orange lump of cheese. In the middle was a plate with twenty slices of bread and butter, two piles of ten. When Mrs Garter poured the tea the girl nearest her put milk in each mug, and the next girl administered one spoonful of sugar to each one and stirred. There was a plate with nine yellow squares of sponge cake, and in front of a little blond boy's plate sat a chocolate iced cupcake wrapped in silver foil. It turned out that he was Jeremy, Mrs Garter's own son. "I'm sorry for them," said Mrs Garter, "but bringing my own boy up just as miserable isn't going to help anyone." Besides cupcakes, Jeremy was allowed into the kitchen, and on to Mrs Garter's pink lap.

Opposite Emma sat a boy of about fifteen. He had a pale bony face, with a semi-circle of red spots under his mouth. His short sandy hair stood on end. He chewed with his mouth open, like a sheep. He didn't look at her. Mrs Garter started to talk about him when she'd finished with Delia. Anthony Childs. He was a lazy one. He didn't lift a finger at school and he'd live to regret that, she knew. He seemed to think that food and a roof over his head were his right, he'd have a rude awakening when he was sixteen, what did he think would happen then? He couldn't stay here forever. The boy chewed stolidly on, ignoring her. Emma pushed her chair back from the table in an attempt to disassociate herself from Mrs Garter, who appealed to her, "They've got no idea some of them, you know, he's in cloud-cuckoo-land, isn't he? He hasn't even thought about a job, he has it too easy here, that's the trouble."

Emma stared at the table cloth. It was generally possible to silence people by refusing to make eye contact with them. But not Mrs Garter. The meal was endless, the woman's easy voice running on over the unnaturally loud sounds of children chewing and swallowing and

45

slurping their tea. Self-consciously Emma cradled her cup in her hands, wondering if there would be an inquisition over the last uneaten slab of cake (which must have been intended for her). Impossible to imagine a week of such meals, let alone six months. Impossible that she could willingly be here.

But she had chosen it. She had a university place a year away, and two impulses determined that she spent the interim here rather than travelling to India or making as much money as possible. The first was pure indignation at the state of the world. Some people were starving to death while others had too much; people were being terrorized and killed in wars which were not only expensive but also totally pointless. Politicians spent billions of pounds on horrible weapons, while people were hungry, illiterate and ill. At thirteen, Emma's intention had been to learn as many foreign languages as possible, then set off on a round-the-world mission to explain to all heads of government, in simple terms that they would be able to understand, why it would be better for everyone if they stopped building weapons and fighting, and started to be nice to each other. Now she was eighteen, it seemed she had been a little arrogant, and she was aware that her impulse to set the world to rights was old-fashioned and in slightly bad taste. But enough of it stayed with her to prompt her into "something worthwhile—helping people in some way—" for her year off.

The second impulse was a newer one; guilt. Recently she had discovered that she was privileged and middle-class. This humiliated her and made her angry with her parents. It put her on the wrong side, and she hadn't asked for it. At least she came from a broken home, that was something. She wanted to meet working-class people—people whose lives were *real*, not cushioned by banknotes and hypocritical etiquette. Mrs G. was a disappointment, though. Would a real working-class person have a pink frilly skirt on her dressing table? Emma thought not.

She endured the evening; when all the children had finished eating one asked to be excused and Mrs Garter gave permission. They all vanished except two girls who started to stack the plates. Emma sat awkwardly still, not helping for fear of upsetting some unknown balance of chores. Mrs G. asked her kindly about herself, and Emma gave her stiltedly bare details. Once she caught the eye of the older girl as she was picking up the heavy teapot, and smiled, but the girl showed no recognition. The children spent the evening clustered in hostile silence around the TV. Emma's cardboard face could no longer even smile. Mrs G. dismissed her before bath time, directing her to her room in the house opposite. Another assistant houseparent and a teacher lived there. Emma's room would be the downstairs back. Mrs G. found her the key and gave her a pair of clean flannelette sheets. I haven't spoken to one of them, Emma thought, but she was weak with relief at leaving the house.

Her room was full of dark utility furniture, a square dressing table and chest of drawers. Mechanically she unpacked her clothes. There were not enough coat-hangers. The kitchen was empty and unused. Well, she would not be eating here, would she. She remembered the tea table suddenly and vividly, then closed her mind firmly. It would be all right. Before she went to bed she phoned her mother from the coin box at the corner to tell her she had arrived safely.

Chapter 10

The next day Mrs G. gave her a pink nylon housecoat too, and told her about the children. Emma quickly confused the problems belonging to each child—bed-wetting, temper tantrums, thumbsucking, allergies, hay fever, nightmares, sleepwalking, truanting from school, smoking, dandruff, eczema, athlete's foot—the lists were endless. She listened unwillingly. It was obvious to her that many of these problems were due to the upsets the children had suffered and that pills and potions and clean towels every day couldn't help at all. It was a pity, she decided, that someone with Mrs G.'s responsibilities should have had no psychiatric training. She flounced upstairs to do the bedrooms, while Mrs G. went shopping. With energetic efficiency she dragged the heavy bunkbeds from the walls and swept the lino. Then leaning on the broom and catching her breath, she examined her surroundings.

The room was bleak. The floor was covered in mustard-coloured lino with a scratchy pattern of thin brown lines. The woodwork was matching chocolate brown, and the walls papered with a yellow floral pattern. A muffled light entered the window through heavy net curtains. There were two double bunkbeds, reminding her of youth hostels, with their air of having supported innumerable lumpen tired bodies. They were made as neatly as hospital beds. On each, there were two grey blankets and a dark blue bedspread. How had children made beds like that? She wondered who slept in which. There were no signs of individuality. Beside each bed was a locker, with labels stuck on each drawer. *Marcus underwear. Leroy shirts*. She opened them and looked at the grey socks and white underpants. Each drawer contained what it said, clean clothes neatly folded. The tops of the lockers were bare. She looked in the small wardrobe. There were coats and a school blazer and two pairs of gym shoes. On one side of the window stood a straight-backed kitchen chair. There was nothing else in the room. The walls were bare, no personal possessions anywhere. She felt under the pillows—not a book or an old teddy or even a packet of cigarettes.

It was worse than a prison. Who expected children to live like this? She burned with indignation. They could put posters on the walls, couldn't they? The children's own drawings, if nothing else. They could surely afford a few books? Didn't they own anything? Things that children collect don't cost money. She thought of her own bedroom, still littered with treasures gathered on walks and holidays—shells, pebbles, fir cones and bits of driftwood. OK, they hadn't got snowflake paperweights or a collection of foreign coins, but they could have something, surely? Emma dusted the clean bare surfaces, heaved the beds back into position and stood to survey her work. It was a room unsoftened by any human touch whatsoever. The girls' room was the same, except the bedspreads were deep pink. Emma wrinkled her face in contempt.

When the children came home from school, she felt more confident than the previous evening. Things would change. They wouldn't live like battery hens while she was around. Susan, a pale skinny girl aged seven, and Delia came back first. They were sent upstairs to change their clothes.

"Can I take them out?" Emma asked Mrs G.

"Yes, if you want—tea's at 5.30. They can show you the neighbourhood, can't they?"

Nervously Emma waylaid the girls as they came downstairs. "Would you like to go for a walk?" Delia stared at her as if she were a post, and Susan burst into

49

giggles. "Shall we go out? You can show me where your school is, and the shops." Emma was very conscious of Mrs G. in the background, overhearing.

Susan shook her head.

"Don't you want to go? Come on, it'll be fun."

"Put your coats on you two and don't keep Emma waiting," interjected Mrs G., and they ran into the kitchen. Emma was embarrassed. They obviously didn't want to go. She would feel an idiot dragging two unwilling children down the street. She didn't say anything else until she'd got them on the pavement, out of Mrs G.'s hearing.

"Don't you want to go for a walk?"

Delia looked at her expressionlessly, then suddenly said, "No."

"Oh." Emma glanced helplessly back at the house. "Oh, well—what do you want to do?"

"Skipping," said Susan.

"Skipping?" Susan started to giggle and whispered to Delia. "OK. Well, have you got a rope? A skipping rope?" Susan ran back to the house.

"Where do you skip?" Emma asked Delia. Delia began to pull leaves off the privet hedge. "Delia, do you skip in the garden?" The child continued to ignore her. Emma squatted beside her. "Delia, listen. We're going to play skipping. Shall we go in the back garden?" Delia looked at her as if she were an irritating insect, and walked slowly towards the house, throwing privet leaves at the ground as she went. Emma stood up, chewing at a fingernail. What now? There was a noise from the house—Mrs G. tapping the kitchen window. Heavily, Emma went to see what she wanted.

"What's the matter?" Mrs G. mouthed.

"We're not going for a walk, they want to skip," said Emma. Mrs G. shook her head, as if to say Emma should know better.

Emma smiled brightly. "I like skipping."

50

Susan emerged with a rope and they went round to the bald lawn at the back of the house. Susan tied one end of the rope to the french windows and backed away holding the other. Delia obediently stood in the middle and jumped as Susan began to turn the rope. There was nothing for Emma to do. She leaned awkwardly against the fence, then went and squatted beside Susan, almost overbalancing as she did so.

"That's very good, Delia. Can you both skip together?" Susan stopped turning and gaped at her. Emma intensified the enthusiasm in her voice. "Look, I can turn and you can both skip together, can't you?" Susan looked dubious. "Try!"

Susan went and stood next to Delia. She was quite a bit taller, startlingly fair next to the black girl. Emma started to swing the rope.

Susan jumped and Delia didn't. "I can't see," she muttered.

"Come and stand in front of Susan, then." They swapped places, and after a couple of false starts, got going well. Nobody said anything. Emma's arm was already aching, she stood turning the rope mechanically, watching the four feet push off from the ground and land again—thud, thud-thud, thud, thud-thud. What a stupid activity. As she continued to turn to the regular thud and lash of the rope on the ground, the skipping seemed infinitely sad. She watched the two pairs of feet straining up to tiptoe and pushing off from the ground, to fall back again immediately. Susan skipped lightly but Delia always thumped down, landing jarringly. Emma watched her taut skinny ankles taking the strain. She wished Delia could have wings and take off.

Both girls were panting. "Do you want a rest?"

Susan shook her head. "Go on—till—one of us—is out!" she gasped. Delia turned to face Susan, and they continued jumping.

It seemed as if she had been turning the rope for hours.

51

Emma's arm was in agony. "You're both too good, we'll have to stop." The girls remained facing one another, while Emma rubbed her arm and swung it by her side. "What do you want to do now?" she asked brightly. Delia started to walk away. "Delia! Where are you going?"

"To watch telly."

"Well—what—" Emma scrabbled desperately for something to suggest. Once they went in to the TV, she would have lost them for the evening. "What about me? That's not fair, is it? What about letting me have a skip?"

Susan took a step towards her. "Can you skip?"

"Yes, of course I can."

"How old are you?"

"Eighteen." Susan started to giggle. "Come on," said Emma, "your turn to hold the rope for me." She positioned herself in the centre and saw through the corner of her eye that Delia had drifted back to watch. Susan turned the rope sharply and it lashed Emma's neck. It hurt. "You'll have to move closer, else it won't go over my head—here—that's it." The rope began to turn again. Now it was too slack for Susan's height and dragged slowly along the ground under Emma's feet. She jumped over it. It seemed to be going terribly slowly.

Susan began to count. "One, two, three, four, five, six . . ."

Emma was breathing heavily. Something moved behind Delia, and the boy came into the garden—the oldest one. He stared for a moment, and Emma flushed. He would think she was an idiot. He vanished. She ran out of the turning rope. "That's enough. I'm puffed." She smiled, and Susan actually smiled back. Delia followed the boy into the house.

"The others are home from school," Emma said cheerfully. Susan looked at her. "I've just seen Anthony," Emma explained.

Susan giggled.

"What's the matter?"

"He's called Orph."

"Anthony?"

"Yes, he's called Orph."

"Orf?" Susan nodded. "Why?" There was no reply. "Is it his nickname?"

Susan smiled.

"Do you all call him that?"

"Yes. He gets mad if we call him Anthony. He's called Orph."

"Ah." Emma was immensely pleased with this breakthrough. She untied the skipping rope for Susan and followed her into the house.

Mrs G. was buttering bread. "You can make some tea," she told Emma. "What happened to your walk?"

"They didn't want to go."

Mrs G. pursed her lips. "You mustn't give in to them," she said. "They're not used to it—they're not like ordinary children, they need to be told what to do." She paused. "Or they can make life very awkward for you, you know—they need to know there's some discipline. It's security for them, you see—and they'll walk all over you if you don't make a stand." Emma counted spoonfuls of tea in silence. "I hope you'll take it as it's meant dear, I just don't want to see you making trouble for yourself— that Susan's a little minx, she'll mess you about something shocking if you don't put your foot down."

Emma could not restrain herself. "But surely, they don't have to go for a walk if they don't want to."

"They don't know what they do want," said Mrs G. simply. "And they certainly don't know what's good for them—do they, my chuck?" she added to Jeremy as he came in.

"What?"

"Know what's good for them."

"Who? The kids?"

"Mmmmmnn." Mrs G. had lost interest and was spooning jam out into a dish.

53

"How old are you, Jeremy?" asked Emma.

"Six."

Her irony was lost on both of them. "And how old is Orph?"

"Orph?" Mrs G. raised her head from the jam and shook it as if Emma had used an obscenity.

"Anthony . . ." faltered Emma. "Susan told me—"

"It may be," said Mrs G., "but I don't see afflicting the poor child with it here as well."

Emma blushed. "Why—what does it—?"

"They call him that at school, some of them, you know—I sent a note about it once but it doesn't do any good."

"But, what's it from? It's nothing to do with his name?"

"Orphan," said Mrs G. shortly. "Some bright spark thought it was funny and started calling him Orphan— they wrote it on his shirt in felt tip and in his books—the shirt was ruined—I sent a note about it, but I don't think the teachers can do much."

"So they call him Orph for short?"

"They do, but not in my hearing. I've told them it's not funny."

"But does he mind?"

"Him? he doesn't care about anything, he doesn't care for man or beast, he'll be behind bars before long." There was silence. Mrs G. sighed. "But that doesn't mean he has to be given outlandish names, even if he hasn't got the sense to mind—and I've told them so." She stamped off to the dining-room with a pot of jam in each hand. Emma was surprised by the depth of feeling she betrayed. If she thinks he'll end up behind bars, why does she care what he's called? It wasn't logical, though it did show that the woman had some sort of a heart. Orph. The boy intrigued her.

54

Chapter 11

Mealtimes were appalling. Over the silence of chewing and the clinking of cutlery Mrs G. brazenly discussed the children as if they were cattle at an auction. "What are you smirking about, Leroy Atkins? Just look at him, you'd think butter wouldn't melt—we know better, don't we? Have you told Emma about that nice new parka you 'found' at school?"

The boy blushed and smiled foolishly, as if she were genuinely praising him for an achievement.

Mrs G. shook her head. "You're too like your dad for my liking, young man—how many times has he been inside now—eh?"

The boy coughed. "Four."

"Yes and there's no need to grin about it either," she said sharply, "if you had any sense he'd tell you it's not much fun—you want to turn your hand to an honest day's work and earn the money for a parka, if you're so keen on them, you want to pull yourself together my boy."

Emma sat back from the contaminated table. What right did the woman have to humiliate them publicly? What did it have to do with Leroy anyway? Nothing. He and his father were separate people. It disgusted her, and there was nothing to do but sit and listen. The children didn't show that they minded. In fact they seemed self-consciously pleased to be singled out for attention. But it was always the same—reminding them what they were and where they had come from. As if they were being firmly planted in deep concrete. It was possible to be anything, do anything. She could be a singer, doctor, politician, artist—anything. And so could

55

they. They were new people, separate people—everyone was; that glittering array of possibilities was their birthright.

Mrs G. seemed very fond of Marcus who was thirteen. One day he brought back a wooden teapot stand that he had made at school and they all admired it throughout tea time. "He's a nice steady worker, and it'll pay off," said Mrs G. in her manner of speaking about them as if they weren't there when they were. "You should see his reports—I'll show you them, they're lovely. All his teachers say he tries hard. He's not brilliant, well, we can't all be, can we?" (Emma was conscious of the barb in this.) "But he tries his hardest, well, what more can you ask? And he'll get good references when he leaves that school, which is more than some other people sitting round this table Anthony Childs." She peeled a cupcake. "No, considering what Marcus has come from I think it's a miracle—I do really."

This did not please Emma either. It wasn't a miracle at all. It was perfectly natural. She was cloyed with embarrassment. It was as if Mrs G. was confidentially discussing the antics of a pet. She hated the association between Mrs G and herself; the children would think them the same, it would be impossible for them to relate to her differently. But how could she dissociate herself? Only by leaning back from the table and not answering. Mrs G. did not take hints. Emma became continuously conscious of what she was not. Not like Mrs G. And not anything consistent with the children—since their responses to her were far from consistent. What she was she did not know.

After a week Susan suddenly became embarrassingly affectionate. She would creep up to Emma sitting stiffly in front of the TV and grasp her hand. "I love you!"

Emma was touched and awkward; she stroked the girl's straggly hair and whispered, "And I love

56

you, Susan," hoping that Mrs G. would not hear.

Susan followed her around everywhere, insisting on holding her hand. She relayed Emma's words to the others: "Emma says we're going for a walk. Who's coming?" "Emma wants the bread, Leroy." "Emma says we must take our wellies."

Of course it didn't help with the others, as Emma was only too aware, and Susan seemed happiest just mooning around her, combing her hair or having soppy nonsensical conversations which Emma couldn't join in. "My mummy's got the biggest house. She lives in a palace, like the Queen. And she's got all—loads of white dresses. All white and silver, she's got cupboards and cupboards full. And jewels."

Emma would smile and say, "That's nice." What else could she say?

Mrs G. obviously took a dim view of it, and said kindly one day, "There's no point in letting them get too fond, dear, it only upsets them when you go."

Emma was humiliated. She *would* go, this was simply six months "off" for her—and she was encouraging the poor child's affection to make herself feel better. Susan would just be hurt. Emma was guilty at the pleasure the girl's attachment gave her, but aware that there was something not at all right about it. Susan seemed to be regressing, becoming more and more childish. She would play with Emma's fingers as they sat watching telly, making them talk to each other in baby talk. "Ickle piggy say, me hungry mummy. Naughty, naughty, no more sweeties today, waa waa—wanty sweetie—" tapping the two fingers together to register a smack. She wanted Emma to herself, and planned little games and outings involving the two of them. But Emma was determined not to appear to have a favourite. She must get through to the others.

The others were not in the least interested in her bright attentions. Tracy, the oldest girl, ignored her

57

coldly. She suggested to Leroy and Marcus that they do some drawings or paintings for their walls. They looked at her as if she was mad. One day Delia brought home from school a blobby blue mess on a big sheet of paper. Emma enthused and went to put it up. Delia and Susan stood in the doorway watching her.

"What's that?" asked Susan. There was silence.

"Go on, Delia, tell her what it's a picture of."

"It's—it's—it's a BOTTOM!" shouted Delia.

"It's stupid," decided Susan. "I'm going to throw it away."

"Oh no you're not," said Emma.

"It's my wall," said Susan.

"No, it's not."

"It's near my bed."

Emma sighed. "Listen, Susan, this is a big wall and there's room for lots and lots of pictures. I've told you, if you want to draw some pictures we'll stick them on the wall too. Next to this one. Or here. See, there's plenty of room."

Susan snorted.

"D'you want to do a picture?"

"I do," said Delia.

"Go and sit at the dining table, both of you, and I'll get some things." She found paper and pencils. There were some paints in little pots, but they were all dried up. When she had got the girls organized she gouged the paint out of the pots into saucers, and started mixing one up with water.

"Here." Susan thrust a scribbled-on piece of paper under her nose.

"Mmmn. Very nice. What is it?"

"I don't know," said Susan.

"Oh, well, it's not finished is it?"

"Yeah, put it on the wall."

"Come on, Susan. You can do better than that. Do a really nice one for the wall."

58

"It is nice. Put it up. You put up hers."

Emma mashed at the lumps of paint with a fork. "Look, you've only spent about two minutes on it. Do something carefully. Do a picture of somebody. Do a picture of yourself."

Susan stamped back to the table, and there was an angry shout. Emma hurried out of the kitchen. Delia had used five or six sheets of paper, putting a huge scrawl on each then throwing it on the floor. "See, look what she's doing."

"Delia!" Emma picked up the papers and took away the remaining blank ones. "That's silly, you're meant to do a picture, not just a horrible scribble. Draw something nice. We're not putting that on the wall, it's a mess."

Delia looked at her coldly.

"Colour it in. You've hardly used the paper at all—look at all this blank space. I'll give you some paints in a minute, when they're ready." She went back to the kitchen and continued to mash the paints, listening for further argument.

Leroy suddenly came in. "What're you doing?"

"Mixing up these paints. Do you want to do some painting?"

He looked over her shoulder. "OK."

"Well, they're all lumpy. Try and mix this one." She handed him a saucer of green and he attacked it with a fork. Susan was shouting again. It was beginning to feel as if things were out of control. Emma noticed that both she and Leroy were making little spatterings of paint on the floor. Marcus appeared. "Leroy, do it over the sink—look, we're making a mess."

"Can I do some?" asked Marcus. She gave him her saucer and went to see Susan and Delia. Delia was stabbing her paper with the pencil, marking the table through it. Susan was working diligently on a minute blotch in the corner of a sheet of paper. Emma gave Delia a newspaper to rest on and admired Susan's creation.

As soon as she did so, Susan stopped. "It's finished."

"But what about all this? It's a shame, can't you draw something else here?" Her voice lacked conviction. She had given them drawing materials so they could express themselves. Susan's squitty little blobs and Delia's scribbles were perfectly valid expressions of their feelings, weren't they? "No, all right, we'll put it up. It's very nice. Are you going to do another?"

There was a shout and scuffling noise in the kitchen. She hurried to the door. Marcus was crouched behind the washing machine, shielding his head; Leroy was standing over him with a forkful of paint. As Emma stepped forward he flicked it onto Marcus's head.

When Emma finally chased them out of the kitchen, it, and they, were covered in paint. Delia had gone off; only Susan sat, labouring over yet another tiny blob in the corner of another blank sheet of paper. Emma cleaned the kitchen. Mrs G. was due back at six. Emma buttered the bread. The boys weren't in the garden. She didn't know where they had gone. She hated the idea of them coming back in those clothes. But it would be impossible to wash them without Mrs G. seeing. Natural enough for children to get dirty when painting, wasn't it? Not if they hadn't painted at all. Not if they hadn't put on one of the eight old shirts that hung on hooks in the hall specifically for that purpose. Not if she had screamed at them to stop and they hadn't. No one had even enjoyed the painting session. Emma was close to tears. Mrs G. wouldn't say anything about their clothes, but Emma couldn't bear her to see the evidence of her own incompetence.

She went to the dining-room. "We'll have to pack up for tea now, Susan. You have done a lot. That's nice. What is it?"

"It's you."

"Ah." Emma looked at the scratchy little black thing.

60

It reminded her of a piece of barbed wire. "Haven't I got a head?"

"There." Susan pointed to a minute dot at the end of one barb.

"OK. Let's go and put them up." They gathered up the drawings and went upstairs. Not knowing where Leroy and Marcus were gnawed at Emma's stomach. What if something happened? What if they said something to Mrs G.? They might still be fighting—she hadn't been able to stop them.

She spread the drawings on the bed. There were fourteen of them, all terrible, shapeless, colourless scribbles. It was ridiculous to put them up. "What shall we put where?" she asked Susan. Susan chose where they should go. Delia's sheets were scrumpled and torn where she had stabbed her pencil through. The final effect was of litter stuck to the wall.

Mrs G.'s return restored order. The children reverted to being meek and law-abiding. They sat obediently around the table eating their tea in silence, while Mrs G. chatted about her visit to her sister. The paint was not mentioned. Emma felt as if she had put the lid back on to a basket of snakes. She was not pleased with herself. But she was even more angry with them. Couldn't they see it was to their own advantage to be a little more human?

Chapter 12

The house ran like clockwork, in ways which Emma either detested or failed to notice. The children obeyed a bath rota, a table-laying rota, a dishwashing rota. There were set days for changing clothes, washing hair, cutting nails. For Emma and Mrs G. there was a cleaning rota, a washing day, an ironing day, a shopping day, a time for cleaning the windows and a time for sweeping the path. 11 a.m. was time for coffee.

They sat in the kitchen, on either side of the wide table. The window was steamed up on the inside. Outside it was raining. It added to the air of conspiracy which Emma always felt when the children were out and they were alone in the house. She hunched over her coffee cup, blowing so that the warm steam enveloped her face. It was pleasant to be grown up and not at school. "What happens to them when they leave here?"

"The children?"

"When they're grown up I mean, do you keep them after they leave school?"

Mrs G. shook her head. "They leave when they're sixteen or at the end of school if that comes later—then it depends—there are a couple of hostels where most of them go for a bit." She gulped at her coffee. "They can be more independent, you know, they have their own room and cook for themselves, there's a warden ... and the social workers still keep an eye on them—"

"And what about the others? If they don't go there?"

"Well, it's up to them—if they can find somewhere else to live, fair enough, I mean, they're old enough to get married, aren't they? They're on their own—they're adults, supposedly."

Emma played with her coffee spoon. "The ones you've had—do they all get jobs?"

Mrs G. shook her head. "Some do. They don't always keep them though—I lose touch with some of them." Emma was surprised that she kept in touch with any of them. Mrs G. told her about Kathy who had got married at seventeen to a lovely man, and brought her baby to show Mrs G. "But a lot of them—just don't—I don't know—they don't get anywhere. There's no go in them somehow, not like a normal kid, they always end up following the leader, can't think for themselves—and they usually latch on to someone who'll do them no good.

62

It's the old story—they end up inside. Well Leroy will, I mean, it runs in the family doesn't it?"

Emma swallowed the last of her coffee, although it was too hot. How could the stupid woman expect them to have "go" if they'd never been allowed to make a decision in their lives? How did she expect them to cope with independence when every solitary thing was done for them, even to measuring out a capful of Squeezy for the washing up? How were they supposed to learn to cook? Or shop? Or wash clothes? Never mind know when they wanted to go for a walk. She was so indignant she could not begin to argue. And Leroy would end up inside, would he, because of his dad?

"And then they have children," said Mrs G., "and history repeats itself—they don't know how to be parents—well how can you expect it?" She spoke more slowly, staring into her coffee cup and tilting it gently from side to side so that the dregs trickled across the cup. "It seems wicked, I know, but I can't help thinking, sometimes—well, that it would be kindness to sterilize them, you know." She waited but Emma didn't speak. "It does run in families, it's bound to—look at a girl like Susan—her mother's no more than a prostitute. She's taken the girl out four times since I've had her, and each time it's been a different man in a fancy car. Susan's already enough of a madam—wait till she's old enough to fling herself at anything in trousers—she'll be pregnant by the time she leaves school—maybe she'll have an abortion—I could get her put on the pill—well, all right, but she'll still manage to get herself pregnant—she'll never look after the children properly, she'll be all over them one minute and bashing their heads against the wall the next—by the time she's twenty I bet I'll have a couple of hers in here, if I'm still going." She laughed shortly.

Emma continued to stare at the table top. I won't look at her. But she couldn't help herself. "You might as well shoot them now."

There was silence. Mrs G. looked at her levelly. "No, dear, that's not what I said." She got up, without haste, and went upstairs. Emma continued to stare at the table until her eyes were smarting. Why is she here, then? Her rage at Mrs G.'s wickedness slowly drained away to leave the discomfort of having offended somebody. And somebody that she still had to work with. Well, so what? Obviously she, Emma, wasn't adult enough to understand the fine moral distinction of it being OK to sterilize them because such people shouldn't exist, but not OK to shoot them. Which seemed to be more honest. Why should one be right and the other wrong? She was conscious of sullenly clinging to her argument because she could not understand Mrs G. She could not see how the woman could do her job or want to do her job if she really thought it hopeless. There was no obvious reason for doing it. It wasn't exactly well paid.

Chapter 13

Mrs G. was markedly cooler towards her after that, and at first Emma was relieved to be spared her confidences. But the children continued to treat her with quite arbitrary affection and indifference, and it was hard not to feel steadily liked by anyone. In her time off she read and wrote letters and went for walks. She was determined not to rush home at the first twinge of unhappiness. But she began to feel slightly unreal. She wanted Mrs G.'s friendliness again, the remark about shooting them haunted and humiliated her. Emma went round in circles. On some days everything seemed possible. She was doing things with the children which Mrs G. didn't do; she did have hope for them. It would make a difference.

One Saturday she took the three youngest girls shopping. Mrs G. never took them, and obviously thought it a bad idea, though she said nothing. Susan was in a very good mood, officiously carrying the shopping bags and mothering the others. The sun shone brilliantly, it was one of those clear autumn days when light seems brighter and sharper than it ever is in summer. The sky was clear dark turquoise, and even on that drab estate the odd bush had yellow-tinged leaves. In the supermarket Susan wheeled the trolley alongside Emma, and Delia and Rose trailed behind staring at the shelves. Emma was happy, watching Susan select packets from the shelves and place them reverently in the trolley. They negotiated the trolley with exaggerated caution past old ladies and boys stacking groceries.

At the checkout counter Susan packed the two shopping bags while Emma paid. Delia and Rose were still on the other side of the counter. "Come on, you two." Outside in the sun again, Emma realized that they had not come on. "Go and get them Susan, there's a good girl."

Susan rushed back, and Emma winced at the volume of the call—"Deeelia! Ro-ose!" After a minute she returned. "They won't come."

"For heaven's sake. Hold these." Emma went in and saw them at the other end of the shop. She'd come in the exit and couldn't get through. She went outside again and round, walking quickly past the hesitating tempted shoppers so that they looked up nosily. Rose saw her first and gave a little squeal of excitement. Then she grabbed Delia's arm and they started to run up the aisle. "Rose!" Emma called in a low voice, but the urgency in her tone made everyone stop what they were doing and look up. Feeling a complete fool she followed them up the aisle, knowing full well that they would turn and run down the next—which they did. The shop froze around them; people squeezed themselves and their trolleys into the side and stared with distaste at the wild disobedient children.

Emma turned halfway down the aisle and went back to catch them at the other end. Rose ran straight into her, squealing with excitement. Emma grabbed her arm viciously and hauled her towards the exit, looking back once to check that Delia was behind. She felt every eye in the crowded shop following them out, scorning her for an incompetent who couldn't control her children, listening to see how she would tell them off.

Susan was standing guard over the shopping. Emma lashed backwards and grabbed Delia's arm, so that she had hold of both of them. "Bring the shopping please Susan." She walked quickly on, to get as far away from the shop as possible. At the corner she let them go with a little shake. "You are both very, very naughty. I'm not going to take you shopping again. *Ever.* D'you hear? Because you don't know how to behave. I'm very cross with you." Then her anger evaporated, and she was standing there foolishly with Delia staring at her blankly and Rose's face crumpling into tears. How should they know how to behave? It had been her fault. Now they were all upset.

"You are *naughty!*" Susan suddenly scolded from behind her. "You can't come with me and Emma *any* more." Rose's preparations for crying came to a conclusion in a long drawn-out bleat.

"All right, Susan, that's enough. I've told them off and that's the end of it," Emma snapped at her and bent to wipe Rose's eyes. "Come on, Rose, stop crying. But you mustn't do that again—promise?" Rose snivelled for a while then nodded. "And you Delia, eh?" Emma did not look too carefully, knowing there would be no reaction. "Well, come on then." She took each of their hands, Rose offering hers blindly, and Delia making no resistance when hers was taken. "Come on, Susan."

They went fifty yards before Emma noticed that Susan

66

wasn't following. She turned and waited. Susan was standing perfectly still, with a shopping bag in each hand, staring after them.

"Come on." Emma made her voice light and encouraging. Perhaps the bags were a bit heavy. The street behind Susan was empty, glaring grey. All the pavements here were far too wide, as if they expected crowds and must be continually disappointed. Susan approached a few steps then stopped and put down the bags. "Come *on*, Susan!" Nothing happened. The road seemed to undulate, further up, in the glare of the sun. "Bring the bags here and I'll carry them." Suddenly she realized with horror that Susan's face was contorting itself.

"NO!" The shout was impossibly loud. The air shook, the street shook, it was enough to waken every dead soul in the place.

"Susan!"

But the bellow was continuing inexorably. "I WANT TO HOLD HANDS."

Emma was running towards her, she must be stopped. How could she shout so loudly? It was impossible. "Stop it! Stop it!" She picked up the two bags, she couldn't hold them both in one hand. Susan was staring at her with red puffed-up face, a mechanical toy all wound up and ready to go off. "I can't hold your hand with all this shopping—come on, don't be so silly, help me carry this one."

No reply.

"Susan! Don't be such a baby. Hold hands with Delia if you can't walk on your own. I thought you were a big girl. I thought you could be a help." Delia and Rose were walking on. She must stop them before they got to the crossing. "Get a move on now, I never heard anything so silly." Her mother's phrases and tellings-off sprang readily to her lips, she could never have found her own words to tell the child off. "Susan!" Like horrible clockwork Susan's face went into motion again. "Susan, stop it—"

"I WANT TO HOLD HANDS!" She didn't even pause for breath at the end but started to scream. It sounded as if her vocal chords would rip at the first shriek. But no—scream after scream, hideously, impossibly loud. Emma dropped the bags and shook her.

"Susan—Susan—" Something awful was happening. Was she having a fit? She squatted and hugged the girl to her, to muffle the sound. "Hush, stop it. Please, hush—" The girl's body was rigid. Time stopped between one awful ripping scream and the next. At last Susan gasped and began to cry, her body went limp and she nearly fell. Emma hugged and squeezed her, rubbing her back and her head, amazed that the child could still cry. She couldn't believe she had made those noises.

Eventually, hooking one bag around her wrist and holding the other, she pulled a weak and weeping Susan along after the others. They had stopped, rooted to the spot by Susan's first scream. Emma squatted down again, disentangling the bag from her wrist where the strap had made a deep purple groove. "Susan, it's all right now." She wiped her eyes, unable to think. "All right—it's all right—ssshhh—" Susan stopped crying easily, and didn't speak. Emma gave Rose and Delia a bag to carry between them and took the other herself, holding Susan's hand with her right. Every house on the estate must have heard that cry. Susan had never—Mrs G. had never told her that Susan could do that. But she must have done it before. She must have done. It wasn't a normal cry. There must be something wrong with her.

Chapter 14

Three and a half weeks passed. Emma was going home for four days. She had to walk through the estate to get to the road where the bus stopped. It was a different sort of road from the estate roads, a gritty blue-black road with cats' eyes down the middle. A real road. On the other side was a dark green field, with heavy purplish clouds above it. The colours were intense. She crossed over and looked back at the estate, with its wide toy roads that no one ever wanted to go along.

The bus when it came was scarlet, against the dark road and green field. She stared out of the windows as if a blindfold had been removed. Far away, two thick rays of sunlight penetrated the heavy cloud and made gold of a newly ploughed field. Most trees were bare now, the perfectly balanced skeletons of branch and twig outlined against the sky, arbitrarily yet painstakingly beautiful. A group of jet-black crows flapped up heavily from the roadside as the bus passed them. She swapped from bus to train. The ticket collector's face was cobwebbily wrinkled in a million fine tiny creases which all moved when he smiled. She hadn't looked at a face for weeks. The train raced through landscapes that leapt into her eyes. Cows, patterned in purest white and midnight black, the vividness of their colouring lifting them off their dark green background. The corn stubble was still being burned off in some places. A puff of blue smoke hung between four hedges, and a hairline of orange flame raced along the ground beneath it, as if trying to escape. The blackened stalks were left behind, still smoking and smoking as if they wouldn't ever die. And out of the fat midlands the countryside bulged and pushed and wrinkled into the northern hills. The moors a colour between mould and yellow, with shadings-in of purple heather, clear cut against the pale blue sky. Streams sparkling like ice in dark green intimate cracks in valleys. The long black tunnel that you come out of suddenly like the day has exploded and the white light shattering blackness has made kaleidoscope green, yellow, blue of earth to fly out in all directions before your amazed pupils.

Back in the village, she walked slowly past crowded, vivid gardens, with the last of the roses leaning crimson against the stone wall here, and a glory of golden chrysanthemums there, so that she snitched a leaf in passing and crushed it for the spicy chrysanthemum scent to stain her fingers. Deep purple michaelmas daisies carried her back to harvest festivals, church and the gloomy brilliant colour and smells of it. A part of her head still held the threadbare thinness she had just left, weighing and contrasting it. She felt ashamed that it was so beautiful. Siberian crab apples on a tree were the colour and shape of flames. And now she could see the side wall and scarlet virginia creeper right up to the slates this year, and fat green quinces ripening on the japonica. Home.

Chapter 15

At 8.30 every morning Orph set out from the house. On some mornings he went to school. It was a ten minute walk through the anonymous streets of the estate to the grey cement and metal edifice that was his school. It squatted behind its wall and car park like a blind monster. Navy-blue clad children approaching it were dwarfed and vanished without trace into its dark doorways. The only splash of colour was provided by the teachers' cars, untidily parked around a bronze sculpture of a lop-sided arrow head balanced on a granite column. The sculpture was eight feet tall. Letters in the granite announced its title to be *Youth Forges Ahead*. It was known familiarly to pupils as "Big Dick".

Orph entered the main gate (forbidden to pupils) and dodged across the car park (also forbidden). He caught the eye of a young woman teacher balancing exercise books on her knee in a yellow Mini; she looked away quickly, unwilling to confront him. As he gained the safety of the doorway a deep bellow penetrated the noise of voices and engines around him.

"Boy! BOY!!" The voice was impossibly loud. There was abrupt silence. "You—bo-oy." Orph took a step backwards and looked up. A scarlet face was staring down from a first-floor window. "What d'you think you're doing?" it shrieked furiously.

Orph shrugged.

"Answer when you're asked a question, you ill-mannered lout."

"Coming to school."

"Coming to school, *sir*. Coming to school how?"

Orph hesitated. "Walking sir."

"Walking? I'll give you walking. You came through the car park, didn't you?"

"Yes sir."

"Are you supposed to come through the car park?"

"No sir."

"Why not? Eh? Why not?"

Pause. "Dunno."

The voice exploded into an even higher pitch of fury. "'Dunno'—you 'dunno', eh? And how long have you been in this school? Four years? Five years? D'you think we make up rules for our own amusement? There's a reason for it, lad, and it's to protect *you*—to stop you getting run over. Pupils are not allowed to walk across the car park.

71

D'you understand? For their own safety. D'you understand?"

"Yes sir," mumbled Orph.

"Well don't do it again. Idiot!" screamed the voice, and the window slammed. Adam Fowles breathed deeply and felt the red draining from his face. Would a performance like that have any more effect on the boy than any other kind of treatment? Unlikely. He was impervious. Adam felt depressed. He consulted the register on his desk. Orph had been absent so far that week; it was a pity he'd come back. Various complaints about him would have to be followed up now he was here.

Orph stepped through the doorway as an electric bell rang shrilly. Gangs who had been leaning against the corridor walls began to shuffle into classrooms. He joined the mob on the stairs, they were packed tightly, pushing each other closer and closer together. A girl in front of him looked round. "Yeuch!" she whispered to her friend, and they giggled, pressing themselves away from him. The glass doors at the top of the stairs were locked. More and more children joined the crowd.

A demented shriek sounded behind Orph. "Come down! Come down, all of you, NOW!" Only a few children heard. They half turned, uneasily, unsure whether they could ignore the voice. The woman began to haul on the collars of the children at the back of the crowd, pulling her way through them. "Go down. Make a line along the corridor and wait. Go down. You can see the door's locked." Her progress up the packed stairway was slow. Gradually they made way for her, pushing each other aside—a few retreated to the bottom of the staircase. When she reached the top step she turned and flourished her keys. "You're a lot of silly *sheep*. Sheep. You've all got eyes—you can see the door's locked." Her voice rose higher, over the giggles and whispers of some of the children. "Go down all of you. Make a line. Go on." There was a lot of muttering. She stood glaring at them. Very,

72

very slowly they began to move into a line. Various insults came to her ears. "Stupid cow. Who does she think she is?"

She stood, red-faced, lips pursed, willing them to get into some sort of line. They were taking ages. She would be late for the sixth form. "Come on. Wake up! A line, I said." It would have to do. "No pushing," she commanded in her high thin voice, unlocked the door, and slipped through smartly herself in order not to have to see the pushing that would undoubtedly follow.

Orph made his way to his classroom, and slumped in a desk near the front. The teacher was apparently absorbed in the register.

A gang of boys lounging on their desks at the back of the room began a low chant. "ORPH-orph-orph-orph-ORPH-orph-orph-orph—".

The teacher looked up. "That's enough."

They stopped.

"Where's your note?" he said to Orph.

"Haven't got one."

"Why were you absent?"

"I was ill." Someone guffawed loudly.

"Then you should bring a note."

"Bring it tomorrow sir," said Orph automatically.

"Make sure you do," replied Adam equally automatically. He knew the boy hadn't been ill. Well, what could he do? There was no point in him coming to school anyway. He checked the register rapidly. "Right. Assembly. Go down quietly please."

There was a chorus of protest. "Oh no. Why?" "D'we have to?" "Oh sir—can't we stay here?"

"I wish we could. The answer's no. Go on—quickly." He watched them shamble-push out of the door. The boys were like a different species, with their big bony heads and pasty colouring, skinny ankles showing between tight trousers and clumsy boots. Orph walked apart from them. They teased him. But who could blame them? There was something infuriating about the blankness of his face. As if he was always laughing at you, secretly.

A small man in a black gown stood on the stage facing the fifth year. They shuffled and fell silent under his gaze. "Take off your raincoats," he said. Parkas were unzipped and slowly removed. Form teachers darted in and out of the rows making sure people obeyed. "Well don't stand holding them!" he snapped. "Put them down. Stand up straight!" A few murmurs of complaint were heard, about coats getting dirty. They subsided quickly. "Now. I have something extremely important to say this morning. So listen very carefully."

"Sir?" A pasty-faced girl whispered to Adam.

"What?"

"Can I sit down? I feel funny." He rose abruptly and gave her his chair. She was always doing this. He stared at her. Did she ever have any breakfast, he wondered. She looked awful. Maybe he would stop her coming into assembly. He shifted his weight wearily and hoped it would be short.

"In a place like a school, lots of people from different homes and different backgrounds are brought together. We don't all agree. Maybe we don't all even like one another. But we try to get on. It's in all our interests to get on, because we all use the same buildings, every day, we have to get on with each other, we have to take a pride in our buildings. We have to pull together, to keep our school nice, to make sure it's a happy place to be, don't we?" He paused rhetorically. The fifth years stared at him, or at the floor, or at the backs of each others' heads.

"This is a lovely building. We're very lucky in this school, we have a lovely new building, with all sorts of luxuries that weren't dreamt of when I or your parents were young. And we must all pull together to keep it nice, we must all take a pride in our building. But— BUT—" the voice sank lower, hoarser, more intimate— "there are some people—not many, they know who they are—some people who don't care about this school. There

74

are some people who are so ignorant and selfish that they don't stop to consider how lucky they are—they don't consider the building, they don't consider the rest of us who use it, they don't consider the taxpayers who pay for it—completely INCONSIDERATE people—who are trying to ruin this school. Inconsiderate, small-minded, disgusting vandals—you know who you are—spoiling things for everyone." He paused for effect, glaring over the heads of the fifth years, who took the opportunity to sniff and cough and shuffle their feet.

"You may have noticed," he began again, "that a certain boys' toilet on the second floor has been closed. You may have noticed that toilet has been locked. And that toilet will remain locked. It will be highly inconvenient for boys using that end of the school. They will not be able to use that toilet; they will have to go downstairs and across the school to the toilets near the gym. Everybody will suffer; there will be more congestion in the corridors. That toilet has been locked because of vandals. Because some people don't care about the rest of us; they don't care about making our school a good place to be. They are stupid, selfish people, who can't think of anything constructive to do with their time and spend it destroying things. They are the kind of people who will end up in prison, very soon. Society has no place for people like that. That toilet will remain locked—LOCKED I say—until those responsible for the graffiti on the walls there own up to it. Then they will clean it off. And they'd better not leave it too long—I've got a very good idea who they are, and if they haven't owned up by four o'clock today, I shall make it my business to HELP them own up."

He stared at them a moment. He's forgotten what he's going to say, thought Adam. But the Head changed his tone abruptly and issued a list of notices and sports results. The bell sounded. "Now, you may go WHEN your form teacher dismisses you—and not before. That

75

boy—you! Go to my office." There was a disorderly stampede towards the exit doors.

Orph pushed and was pushed on his way to the doors. He went into the toilets and had a cigarette. Various people were lounging about there. No one spoke to him. Another bell sounded. He went up the stairs to the second floor.

"You're late," said the teacher.

"Assembly," he said, and sat down.

There were eleven others in the room; it was European studies. The bottom stream did it instead of a language. "Right," said the teacher. "Give these out, please." She handed Orph a pile of dog-eared textbooks and went round the room slapping each person's exercise book on their desk.

"Not that one—I want a new one," said a thin-faced girl as Orph handed her a book. "*That* one." She grabbed at a book, causing him to drop the others. She burst out giggling shrilly. Orph went to his place and sat down.

"Oy—we want some. What about us?" shouted two boys at the back who hadn't been given books yet.

"What are you playing at?" demanded the woman wearily.

"He's chucked 'em on the floor!" shrilled the girl.

The woman spoke with a tired, patient voice. "Pick them up please Anthony and give them out properly." Orph stared at his desk top. "Come on now."

"She made me drop them."

"Well she can help you pick them up."

"I'm not helping him. He's thick." The others were talking and jeering among themselves.

"Anthony, pick up those books and give them out *now*." He sat still. She raised her voice. "If you're not going to do that you can go down to Mr Stanton's office. I'm not going to waste my time with you."

The others whispered and called. "Go on Orph!" "Go and see Stanny—he'll flay yer!" "Chuck 'em at 'er." Orph got up sullenly, flinging his chair back so that it banged against the desk behind. He slammed a book on to each desk.

The boys at the back leered at him. "Thank you, Anthony. Too kind, old chap."

The teacher sighed and smiled unconvincingly. "Thank you, Anthony. What a fuss over nothing. Now turn to page 62." This took some time. One boy insisted that his book didn't have a 62, others wanted to look at things on other pages or dropped their books, seeking a new diversion now that Orph had been put in his place. The teacher stared at them, face glazed, waiting until they were bored enough to do as she had asked. "Right. Capitals. On page 62 there's a list of capitals and important cities in European countries. I want you to copy the list very carefully into your exercise books, so that you can learn it. Look at the page—see, the top one is France. There's a little map showing you where France is. Then there's a list of important towns, Paris, Marseilles, Lyons. Write down the name of the country, comma, then the important towns."

A slight hubbub of noise broke out. Removing her spectacles, she sat down at the desk and started marking some papers. Slowly people opened their books. Two hadn't got pens. She looked up as if she had forgotten them already. "No pens? You are nuisances. Here, I've only got one. Use a pencil."

"Haven't got one." Sighing, she gave him a pencil. "It'll look a mess," he objected.

"It'll look a mess anyway, Wayne, if you write it." The weary voice was suddenly alive with bitterness.

"Cow," whispered the boy loudly.

Orph stared at the page for a while, then started reading the graffiti on his desk top. "Arsenal forever", "Grace and John", "I was here", "Kilroy woz ere", "fuck school", "Jez is a cunt". The others were talking loudly; some were writing, some weren't. The little maps in the

77

book located each European country in relation to the rest by shading it in in a blank outline of the continent.

"Where's England on this?" asked a girl suddenly.

"What?" said the teacher.

"Where's England?"

The woman pulled the book to her. "Here," pointing with a chalky finger. "Don't you even know that?"

"New York isn't on here," complained someone else. "That's a big city."

Slowly Orph began to copy. He copied vertically, making a list of all the countries.

France

Germany

Switzerland

Belgium

The desks and wooden chairs were small. He sat with his knees hunched up between himself and the desk, they wouldn't fit underneath. Wayne hit him on the neck with a paper pellet. He turned and stared with his blank face.

"Got ya, her-her."

"Stop it and get on," said the teacher half-heartedly. Orph laid down his pen, and rested his head on the desk, hands across his neck in case of more pellets. For the remaining twenty minutes of the lesson he semi-dozed, kept awake by the restless mutterings and movements of the others around him. When the bell rang he rose immediately and made for the door.

"Anthony!" shouted the woman. "No one has given you permission to go." As she spoke, the door opened and Mr Stanton, deputy headmaster, appeared. He grabbed Orph by the ear.

"What you doing boy?" Orph twisted and the man shook him slightly. Orph's white face went red, and he turned sharply to face the man.

The woman's apologetic voice broke in: "Ah, Mr Stanton—I was just—"

Stanton looked at the boy with glittering eyes.

"Wanted a word with you, Miss Smart. But it'll keep. I'll have a word with this lout first, I think." The rest of the class were frozen still, half-risen from their desks, fear and humility in their faces. Orph was marched away. They exploded into noise and laughter, and stampeded out of the room, knocking over two desks as they went. Harassed and grey the woman hurried after them, pausing only to right one of the desks.

Stanton had forgotten that there was a parent waiting to speak to him in his office. There was nowhere he could deal with the boy. He backed him up against the wall in the corridor. Children passing gave them a wide berth, leering at Orph from behind Stanton's back. "What were you doing?" he hissed. Orph stared at him wordlessly. "Answer when you're spoken to, boy."

Orph shook his head. "Dunno sir."

Stanton was aware of a whisper behind him. Someone was calling, "O-rph O-rph heh-heh." He checked himself from turning round. This was not a good place for a scene. His legs were trembling. He put his face, with its curiously bright eyes, close to Orph's, and whispered,

"You'd better find out. Think about what you were doing, and you can come and see me at the end of lunch-break. In my office. I don't want to hear 'dunno'. I want to know what you were doing when I came into the classroom." He gave Orph one vicious prod on the shoulder with his index finger. "Go—and think about it." He was frightened of himself as he walked on down the corridor. He hated that boy. Was that what evolution had been for?

Orph remained at the wall, face blank. It was quite easy to believe that he hadn't known what he was doing. A passing boy spat at him. The frothy white glob of spittle hung, self-enclosed for a second on his woollen jumper, then spilt in a long wet dribble down the front of his clothes. Orph leapt away from the wall and after the boy. Children shouted and scuttled to the walls, and the two of them raced along the corridor. The one who'd spat dodged out through a side door towards the tennis courts. Orph rushed after him. He caught him at the far end of the tennis court. The crowd who had witnessed the event were just spilling out of the door after them. Orph swung at the other as soon as he was close enough, and the boy, off balance, fell. Wildly, Orph lashed out at him, flailing with both arms and kicking. His face was contorted. The boy shrieked. Within seconds the other children were there. Five of them flung themselves on to Orph, and dragged him to the ground. The boy who had been down scrambled up. People were screaming encouragement. Orph stopped struggling—his face was blank again, though he was panting, mouth slightly open. With theatrical deliberation the boy Orph had beaten leant over him and spat full in his face. The spittle landed on his cheek and began to slide with gathering speed towards his eye. Orph twisted violently to get up, but five people were holding him.

A boy who had pushed him down glanced at Orph's arm, pinioned to the ground, and took a slow step nearer. Watching Orph's face with smiling curiosity, he raised the toes of his right foot, resting the heel on the ground, and slowly lowered his shoe over Orph's hand. Orph's head turned sharply to the side as the boy, still smiling, transferred his full weight to the foot, crushing the hand beneath. There was a ripple of admiration, mingled with alarm about someone coming, from the back of the mob. They disappeared quickly, those who were holding Orph administering a final kick to his side before leaving. He sat up and scrubbed the spittle from his face with his sleeve. Then he started to pick out the small pieces of gravel embedded in the palm of his left hand.

A woman was hurrying across the empty tennis court. He got up and started walking slowly towards school, his left hand hidden in his pocket. As he approached she slackened her pace, staring at him. "Are you all right?"

He nodded.

She looked at his crumpled filthy clothes and red face. "What happened?"

"Nothing."

She looked him up and down again. He wasn't obviously hurt. And everyone else had gone. They must learn to survive on their own—anyway, he was a big lad, it was time he learned to fight his own battles. She asked kindly, "What's your next lesson?"

"Maths."

"Who's your teacher?"

"Mr Davis."

"Well you go and wash your face, and I'll tell Mr Davis you'll be a little bit late."

He said nothing.

When he arrived at maths, fifteen minutes late, he was greeted by jeers. Mr Davis wasn't there yet. The woman, embarrassed, had given the class the message to give to Davis: "Anthony Childs has permission to be ten minutes late."

"Tell 'er all about it, did yer?" "She bin dryin' yer tears?" "Yer on to a good un there, Orph," and an obscene gesture to indicate the size of breasts. Their faces were creased with mirthless laughter, like the raised muzzles of dogs when the lips are drawn back in a snarl.

Orph was rescued by the arrival of Davis. Silence came clean as a cut when he opened the door. He stood in the doorway staring at them, then went quickly to his desk. The room was quiet, the snarling faces transformed to humble eagerness, looking up at him. "Where's Elizabeth Banks?" People looked around hopefully, as if she might be hidden in a desk.

A girl put up her hand and he nodded at her. "Please, sir, she's got a doctor's appointment." This information was received in silence. He continued to glare around the room. Then with an economical gesture he placed a pile of exercise books on a front desk. He pointed with one

81

finger to a girl at the back of the room, who scuttled forward to give out the books. When she had finished he did the same routine with a sheaf of blank paper and another child. When all were equipped, he remained still as a coiled snake watching them. Under his gaze they shifted in their seats, pulled back their shoulders, tried to sit up straighter and look alert. Nervously they adjusted the position of book and paper on their desks. Gradually his gaze came to rest on a boy sitting near the window. The boy was staring out at a game of football on the far playing field. Moving in complete silence, Davis approached the boy. Every head in the class turned to follow his movements, with the pure pleasure with which they would watch any perfect hunter. Thirty-one breaths were indrawn simultaneously as the hand was raised above the unsuspecting head—the force of the blow caused the boy to shout out in terror. He covered his head with his hands and sat perfectly still. Davis returned to the front of the room, and stared at him. Quickly the boy put his hands in his lap and looked back at Davis.

"Thank you," said Davis quietly. "Page 38. Multiplication revision. Start on page 38 and work through 39 and 40." As if worked by clockwork, the thirty-two pupils opened their books and lifted their pens. Complete silence reigned for the following thirty minutes.

After maths Orph went to English, where they were asked to read quietly a library book selected from the reading box. The teacher was interviewing fifth formers who wanted to take A-level English; a steady stream of them came throughout the lesson. Orph's class talked quietly and inscribed their names and obscenities on the desks and in the library books.

Stanton kept Orph waiting for fifteen minutes before bringing him into the office. "Having a good day, aren't you?" he snapped.

Orph stared blankly.

"Fighting." There was a silence. "What was it about then?"

Orph shrugged.

Red flickered before Stanton's eyes. He had had enough. He continued to stare at the lout, who looked at the ground and mumbled inaudibly. "What?"

"Someone spat at me, sir."

"Why?" It was a stupid question. It was what they did. Animals. They spat at one another. "What were you doing in Miss Smart's lesson this morning?"

"Nothing sir."

"Why not? Didn't you have some work to do?"

"Yes sir. The bell went."

"So?"

"For the end of the lesson."

The trembling in Stanton's legs resolved itself into movement. He took a quick step towards the boy, flexing the cane between his hands. "The teacher decides when the lesson ends. Not you. The teacher." The insufferable blank insolent face stared at him, the pathetic sub-human face of a creature who had no place here—no place at all. "Bend over." And Stanton hit him, impelled by a burning futile rage. The school was full of them. They understood nothing. They destroyed the place. They destroyed the people. Alice Smart had been a good teacher once. He knew how bad she was now. She'd given up. Worn down. By louts like this. Creatures that would never contribute anything to the world. Creatures that could not and should not be educated. Creatures with no future but pain and destruction, for themselves and others. Creatures that should not have been born and should be stopped from breeding. The glitter in Stanton's eyes was scalding. The skin on his face was taut, stretched too tight over the bones. The school was a shambles, worse day by day. Creatures like this. He hit Orph with the passionate hatred that, even a year ago,

83

he would have turned on anyone who voiced such thoughts as his own now.

The boy was white-faced and expressionless when he finished. Stanton's vision was blurred with heat. He turned away in disgust. The boy still stood there. "Go away." Orph walked awkwardly to the doorway. He made his way to the toilets and locked himself in a cubicle. Then he took down his trousers and touched his bare bottom. There was blood. He leaned against the wall, trousers round his ankles. After a while he stooped and lit a cigarette from the pocket, then stood smoking.

The outside door banged open. "Who's in there?" shouted Adam Fowles. Orph stared at the grey toilet door. "You're smoking," shouted Fowles. "I can smell it. Come out immediately."

Orph threw the cigarette end in the toilet and slowly pulled up his trousers. He flushed the toilet and opened the door.

"You. Again." Fowles was really angry. "Very clever. You've thrown it away. Why do you come to school? Why d'you bother?"

Orph shrugged and finally said, "Get told off."

"For not coming? And for coming too, when you behave like this. For heaven's sake, make life a bit easier for all of us. Stick to the rules, boy—it's not for much longer." Fowles turned abruptly.

Orph watched him go, then shuffled along the corridors to the PE department, through the now empty changing rooms and out to the playing fields. Keeping close to the hedge, he walked away from the school. In the centre of the field a group of boys in royal blue shouted and ran together around a ball, united in the game.

Chapter 16

When Emma went back it was as if she hadn't been away. Her identity was blurred; with Mrs G. she was stiff and averted, holding herself away from the woman's cosy friendliness with a deliberate dislike. With the children she was at times a great awkward child herself, trying to join in, not understanding. And at other times, a falsely sweet and enthusiastic adult, trying to honey them into good behaviour or what she wanted, knowing all the time that Mrs G.'s directness was more effective.

Susan wanted to know about where she'd been and what her home was like. When Emma had described the house and garden, and the village it was in, she added brightly, "You'll have to come and stay with me one day, Susan."

"Can I? Oooh—can I?" Susan was overwhelmed with delight. "When?"

Emma was very angry with herself. How? When? What about the other children? Who would pay their train fares? It was an idiotic suggestion, it would come to nothing, except to prove to Susan yet again that she should not believe or trust adults, and that nothing nice could ever happen to her. "It'll have to be when you're grown up, Susan," she lied, knowing she did not deserve that Susan should not tell the others. Of course she did; and Emma solemnly promised Rose and Delia and Leroy that they could come too, when they were grown up. They argued about it, because Susan said she didn't want them to come while *she* was there. And Emma despised herself thoroughly.

All their reactions to her were wrong and arbitrary, they didn't know how to treat her because she didn't know how to treat them. And when they took liberties, she was angry then guilty for blaming them, and everyone was unhappy. Chaos reigned when Mrs G. went out, they stayed up half the night, giggling and screaming from their bedrooms, worked up into such a state of nervous excitement that it could only be ended by slaps and tears.

There was only one who was outside this frenzy. Orph. He took absolutely no notice of her. Whether she addressed him as adult or child, he ignored her. His behaviour under her care did not vary a jot from his behaviour under Mrs G.'s eye. He did not speak to her, just as he did not speak to Mrs G. or to any of the kids. He didn't speak to anyone. He was indifferent. The other kids bellowed and clung and demanded; they liked and hated her until there was not an inch of her life that was not baumed with their sticky fingerprints. Orph was outside it. She came to admire him more and more, as he became more and more defined by his contrast to the others. In the evening watching telly they squirmed around and over her, wriggling across her lap and fighting to sit next to her or to not sit next to her. Orph sat on the floor, still as a corpse, staring with fixed eyes at the screen. If Mrs G. went out and the house became a haunted house of shrill giggles, thuds and loud whispers, Orph was unchanged—in front of the TV or lying on his bunk, silent and motionless in either case. She had to beg and cajole the others into doing their chores.

"Leroy. It's your turn to wash up, isn't it?"

"No."

Emma knew full well it was. "Are you sure?"

"Yup."

"It is his turn. He's a liar." From Susan.

"Shut up snidey pants, none of your business."

"All right, all right. Come on, Leroy, get them done."

"Not my turn."

"Yes it is."

"How d'you know?"

"Because it's Tuesday, it's your turn. Now get a move on." False jollity ringing in her voice. No move from Leroy. "Leroy—come on—then we'll have time for a game afterwards."

"What game?"

"I don't know. What would you like?"

"I don't want to play a stupid game. I wanna watch telly."

"Well, get a move on then." No move. "Leroy, get those dishes shifted now, or there'll be trouble."

"What trouble?" ... and so on.

But on Orph's night, no matter whether Mrs G. was there or not, he automatically cleared the table and washed up with no prompting at all.

When Mrs G. found blood on Orph's underpants she showed it to Emma in exasperation. "Foul, that boy. Disgusting. Always in trouble."

Emma stared. "But it's blood."

"Yes. They have to cane him—only way to make him do anything."

"But blood—"

"He's got no feelings," said Mrs G. simply.

Emma plucked up courage to ask, one day, "Why do they cane you at school, Orph?"

He shrugged.

"Don't you care?"

He shrugged again.

"But it must hurt." She was embarrassed by her questions.

"Yes," he said, not looking at her, and turned on the TV.

Eight days after she came back there was a phone call from Orph's school. Emma answered the phone. They wanted to know where he was.

87

"Isn't he there? Oh no—well what—he must have had an accident—we haven't heard any—"

The dry voice at the other end calmly put her in her place. "I doubt he's had an accident, Mrs—er, Miss—he's only honoured us with his presence for two days of last week. He's up to his old tricks again, I'm afraid. Could I have a word with Mrs Garter?"

Mrs G. took the news grimly. "I thought I'd taught him a lesson last time. It's a waste of time dealing with that boy." When Orph came home, at the same time as the others from school, Mrs G. summoned him into the dining-room and shut the door. Emma sat in the kitchen absently answering various demands from Rose and Susan, her attention focused on Mrs G.'s voice. She could not distinguish any words, but the rise and fall of the voice was hypnotic. As she listened the voice grew louder and angrier, and there was a series of questions to which the answers were inaudible. It seemed as if Mrs G. was arguing with herself or on the telephone. After five minutes there was a shouted question which catapulted Orph from the room. He blundered through the kitchen leaving Emma standing inanely there as if she had been caught listening at the keyhole.

Mrs G. came out slowly. Her face was purple. "Little sod." She sat down heavily. "Not a word—I couldn't get a word out of him." She scowled at the floor for several minutes, then sighed and folded her arms. "Well, if he won't talk he won't—it's his own funeral—he'll find himself somewhere where they make damned sure he's at school because there's nowhere else to go! He won't be staying here."

Emma watched Mrs G., waiting for her to go on. Despite her philosophical words, her face was red and unhappy.

She shook her head. "He's beyond help—hard as nails— he was when I got him—he's beyond help. Not a chink anywhere—stares at you as if you were a piece of furniture."

"Delia's like that," Emma contributed.

Mrs G. looked vague. "Oh—Delia—she'll be all right—but him—no, he's evil, evil—I've got his mark, one day he'll do something and I'll be the only one that isn't shocked. The only one—" She twisted her plump hands unhappily in her lap. "I hope they do put him in a centre—it's no good me having him here, I don't want him now." She looked challengingly at Emma. "And I've never said that before about a child—never."

Mrs G.'s anger with Orph had the same effect on Emma as on the children. They all crept about being exaggeratedly good and helpful. Orph was the only one who seemed unaffected. He returned in time for tea, apparently oblivious to everyone's attention focused on him. He chewed mechanically through one cheese and one jam sandwich and a lump of cake, staring at his plate as he ate. Not that he ever looked at anyone anyway. Emma had never seen him looking directly at her. She stared at him surreptitiously, just as the others were doing, feeling as if she had never seen him before and even now was not seeing properly—as if he were behind glass. She could not decide what he looked like. His sandy hair was short and stood on end. His skin was pale, eyes also pale, a glassy blue. His lower jaw was heavy and wide, his mouth absolutely straight, with no hint of an upward or downward curve. But his face—it was strange. It was the normal collection of features, two eyes, a nose, a mouth. But instead of them together forming a knowable face, they remained individual features because of the lack of any expression which might pull them together. So you could look at his face and, the instant you looked away, not know what he looked like. Because he didn't really look like anything.

They all ate in silence that night, Mrs G. expressing her displeasure by eating with vicious rapidity and leaving the table before any of them. Marcus and Leroy cleared the table and washed up. The others all trooped in to watch TV. Emma went and sat with them. Orph slumped in his usual position, on the floor leaning his back against the middle of the sofa. She noticed that, though the girls sat on the sofa, their knees level with his head on either side, they respected a distance around him, and squashed themselves together rather than risk touching him. Once he had arranged himself, he sat without moving, eyes never flickering from the TV, no expression ever forming on his face. Blank-faced he sat through news, adverts, a comedy serial and a western. Emma considered what she knew about him. He watched TV every night, from 4.30 to tea-time and from tea-time till he went to bed at 10. He never went out. His life consisted of waking up, going to school, watching TV and going to bed. She tried to remember what he did at weekends. He was always there in the evening, watching TV. Sometimes he was out during the day on Saturdays. She had no idea where. But then, he didn't always go to school. Where did he go? Staring at his bony profile, it was unimaginable. Did he go off with friends? She was sure he had none. The children here feared him and rarely spoke to him. He would be no different at school. He had no money, so pubs and cinemas were out, or even amusement arcades. Mrs G. said he would end up behind bars. Maybe he spent the day in criminal activities. A pickpocket? A mugger? Not very plausible.

Over the following days Emma became more and more interested in Orph. The children were all inconsistent, and made her so, but it didn't really matter because their very inconsistency made what she did irrelevant. She wasn't affecting anyone. Her little plots for improving the quality of life in the home, her pet ideas for outings and activities and variety seemed quite arbitrary. Her energy was sapped, she could not face a repetition of the morning she had taken the girls shopping. And anyway, what good did it do? It was a matter finally of getting

through the day without too many crises. And her great
ideas caused nothing but crises. She felt as if huge waves
were constantly crashing down on her and it was as
much as she could do to keep her head above water and
splutter for breath. The routine events in the day took on
a different light—the fixed meal-times and rotas and
tasks to be done. They no longer seemed to imprison the
household and deny spontaneity. On the contrary, they
were nice firm stepping stones over the uncharted depths
and whirlpools of the day. She found herself groping
through the time from 4.30 till tea-time, afraid that the
children might want to do something, hoping for a
mindless trouble-free occupation until the safety of tea-
time could be reached.

And it dawned on her that the children felt exactly as
she did. The security of the definite times and tasks was
vital to them. Little enough mattered in their lives, and
so it was important that they should each make their bed
extremely neatly before breakfast. It was important that
they should exchange their slippers at the back door for
their own pair in the row of outdoor shoes, and replace
the slippers tidily in line. What else mattered? Who
cared? Mrs G. was right. Gradually Emma felt that Mrs
G. was more and more right. Mrs G. created the
children's lives. She had taken from chaos something
which was shapeless and like a painstaking insect she
had woven a form around it. She had spun the strands
that could hold them together, a time for this, a time for
that, lines that should not be transgressed. The
children's lives had shape and therefore, for the first
time, they *had* lives.

Emma came to admire the bedrooms which were
always so safely bare and tidy. The rooms, and the items
of furniture in them, were basic. It seemed to her that
she knew those bedrooms better than any she had known
in her life—and that the children also would always
know them. They weren't disguised and cluttered over

by someone who feared to face the fact that a human animal's needs are simple; it needs to be sheltered and it needs to sleep. The iron bedsteads made curving shadows on the wall when the light was switched on. The tightly stretched covers on the carefully made beds were pleasing, displaying care for order and its attendant comforts. She remembered with disgust her own room at home, the permanently rumpled bed and heaps of assorted clothes littering the chair and floor, the clutter of possessions on every surface. It was the room of a person who cannot face the facts.

As her perspective changed and the stark beauty of the iron bedsteads and neat rows of slippers came into focus, so Orph also came into focus. He was worthy of his setting. Like the furniture, he was present without asserting or intruding. He was simply there. And unlike any human being she had ever known, he never made any kind of demand. He got up and ate and went out and came back and ate and watched TV and went to sleep. He was never different. He was never in a mood or out of it. He never complained, and he had the sense never to be happy. He expected nothing from other people and he was never disappointed.

She began to be obsessed by him. He was heroic. He was the stony-faced cowboy who kills his enemies in a pointless gunfight then rides off alone into the sunset. He couldn't be hurt. If *he* was crucified, he wouldn't cry out so spinelessly and ask why he had been forsaken. He would have expected it. He was self-sufficient, as all the greatest heroes were; the ones who journeyed alone and met with terrible trials and temptations but betrayed no weakness. Men and women who had no need for other people to prop them up. Oddly enough, her father crept into sight here, and she was surprised that she had classified him so. Well, he had rejected her mother and herself; and indeed, in comparison with him, her mother was an emotional parasite. He was a hero too then.

Suddenly her memory crystallized and she realized which hero Orph was above all. *L'Etranger*. She had read the book for French A level and the figure of Meursault had haunted her for weeks. A man who was as perfectly independent and indifferent as a chair. A man made godlike by his lack of need. Orph was Meursault, untouched and untouchable.

Chapter 17

Days and weeks passed routinely. Autumn changed to winter without distinction or remark, except that the rain was more constant and the daylight shorter. Emma watched Orph but learned nothing. She was afraid he would be caught truanting again and get sent away before she had a chance—a chance to what? She wanted to find out something from him. Gradually the time that she still had left to work there stopped being endless, the hump of Christmas was got over and it was a new year. He had still never spoken to her. Nor to anyone else, in her hearing. She had never spoken to him, because she did not know what to say. But she wanted to speak to him.

In February an opportunity arose. Against all the odds in that crowded household, there was an evening when she and Orph were alone with the TV. Mrs G. and Jeremy were out. Leroy, Tracy and Marcus were on a school outing. Susan was in bed with 'flu, and Delia and Rose were in bed because it was bedtime. Emma had been waiting for such an evening. But her shirt stuck to her under the arms and her palms were wet.

She took Susan a drink. Coming back, she closed the door too loudly and stumbled over the mat in her haste to reach the sofa. Avoiding looking at Orph, she stared intently at the TV. Two clean-cut men with guns in their hands were edging along the inside wall of a multi-storey car park. The fair one beckoned the dark one with his gun and they dodged between the cars. The camera moved to men crouched over papers between parked cars. One suddenly raised his head and made a warning gesture. There was a moment of complete silence then the screen exploded with bangs, thuds and screams. The camera selected one of the cops taking a flying leap at a villain, forcing his bead backwards through a car window. Emma instinctively closed her eyes, then glanced at Orph. He was staring expressionlessly at the screen. She glanced at her watch: 8.40. If she sat back she couldn't see Orph's face. But leaning forward was uncomfortable and looked awkward. She twisted the cushion round from her back to her side and sat sideways on the sofa, resting her back against the arm. The positon was still uncomfortable but it would look more relaxed. The TV emitted the sound of a thudding kick and a groan. She glanced at it. The dark-haired cop prodded an inert body with his toe, delicately, as if it might dirty his shoe.

"D'you like this?" Her voice was crackly, she coughed. There was no response from Orph. "Orph? D'you like this programme?"

He turned his head slightly in a quick movement as if to see who had spoken. But his eyes did not leave the screen. "It's OK." The cops were patting each other on the back.

"What's your favourite programme?"

There was a long silence. "Dunno."

"I like those ones about wild life—d'you?" She forced herself to continue. "Where they show lions or something like that, live in the wild. There was an amazing one that showed a lion stalking a zebra and attacking it. Did you see it?"

He nodded.

94

She picked a hair from her cord jeans and placed it carefully on the back of the sofa. And another. And another. She was moulting. She stuck them in a neat row on the nylon stretch cover. When she brushed it accidentally with her fingertips it set her teeth on edge. The programme ended and the news came on. It was much easier to not watch than the cop series. "Don't you ever get bored?"

He shook his head once. He never moved unnecessarily. She looked along his legs, stretched out straight in front of him. Two inches of skinny white calf showed between trouser leg and sock. In anyone else it would have seemed silly, or pathetic. Could he tell she was looking at him? She felt herself turning red. She was only three years older, after all, he might think she was...

She shifted sharply in her seat. This is nonsense. He despises you, you're quite safe. You couldn't be any lower in his estimation. All right then. She was thankful to feel the heat draining out of her cheeks. The question leapt out before she had quite determined it. "Where d'you go when you skip school?"

He did not move. "Depends."

"Ah." She picked at another hair. "What on?" There was such a long silence she thought he wouldn't answer.

"I go to town sometimes. To the precinct."

"Oh."

"Or f'ra walk."

He was either telling the truth or lying. Well, why should he talk to her? She wouldn't expect Meursault to tell her where he'd been. Or even her father. What had she expected? Why ask? She didn't know, but had to carry on, half-way across a tightrope. She hoped the others would come home soon. "Looking forward to leaving school?"

Pause. "Suppose."

"What'll you do?" She realized she had no idea. It had

never even crossed her mind before, what he could do.

"Dunno."

"You going to stay around here?"

He shrugged. "Not bothered."

She counted up the months, March, April, May, June, July. In five months he would have no occupation and nowhere to live. He was not bothered. He was amazing. What would it be like if she was in his place? Mentally she stripped off her encumbrances, one by one: no home to go back to, no village no countryside; no books no records no letters, no diaries no stamp collection no dog; no all of the junk that was hers; no mother, no father, no one expecting her to be anything; no friends to impress, no heaps of glowing school reports, no university place; no O levels no A levels, no neat piles of assimilated books in the brain; no position no plans...

As she stripped them away, she began to get glimpses of an emptiness that must be freedom. How channelled and restricted her life was; there was no way she could ever have been—or become—anything else. They were from different worlds. Her safe little life had been all mapped out for her before she even started. He was on a bigger scale, he could cope with terrifying voids and sit and watch telly without knowing where he was going or when. He was not even shivered by the icy blast of that cold space.

She was ashamed of her little life. How much more he would accomplish than her. How much more he would risk. Without building up little wodges of padding to keep cold reality at bay; without grasping after friends and lovers and demanding recognition and trying to lose himself in other people or "interests" or work. Coolly and evenly he would keep in view his solitude, the facts; his single birth, his inevitable single death, and the intervening futility of three score years and ten. How pathetic people were, scared stiff, all of them, afraid to look it in the face. Afraid of space. And silence.

Girls in glittering body stockings were dancing in a row on the screen. She watched; there was nothing to say. But she wished he wouldn't despise her. It would be better out of this—the other kids, Mrs G., the awful creature they forced her to be. At university she would be free. She would be herself then, like him. And he then...

She saw him standing at the end of July, as if at the end of a long plank which stretched away from her. She could not see what he was facing but it was bright and vague, dazzling like sunlight on water or a snowy arctic landscape. The girls on the screen did the splits and waved bye-bye.

Before Emma left the home, she gave Orph her address in Leesborough. It seemed as if it might be a silly gesture, but the impulse had persisted over several days. She wanted to know what happened to him. She imagined him turning up one day out of the blue, on his way to unknown places. She wanted to see again that vast empty freedom she had glimpsed through him.

She went home finally with enormous relief, conscious of having come nearer to failure in the past six months than she had ever done in any subject at school.

PART TWO

Chapter 18

In late September Emma moved to Leesborough, to be ready for the beginning of term in October. She was sharing a rented house with an old school friend, Alison, who had already been at the university a year.

Emma was ready to enjoy herself, and she plunged uncritically into the bright new world that was on offer. Literally on offer—dazed, she wandered round a great societies fair that offered membership of a seemingly infinite number of groups; social, sporting, political, literary, theatrical, religious—you could choose, as if from blank, what sort of person to be here. And the students offered each other the same challenge, staring at each new face, assessing: who are you, what will you be? A friend? Lover? Someone I want to know? There was a sense of mass exhilaration—escape from home or school or whatever they had been before. Now they were all new, all blazing with potential. It took her a couple of days to adjust to the larger-than-lifeness of it; people extravagantly dressed, theatrically loud, clustered in great gaggles outside bookshops or university buidings, hailing each other from distances as if no one else mattered, dismissing as insignificant all the mere inhabitants of the town, no longer cowed into their petty way of behaving. They, the students, were a majority. They could behave as they wished and set their own standards. And everything was moving, swarming, urgent, everyone who looked at you so greedily was already looking on to the next, we're here, it's here, we're here ... dazzled, blinking, is it real?

At first there was a fantastic sense of power. The place belonged to them. Emma explored her new territory —libraries, lecture halls, cafeterias, bars, union buildings—and the stretch of park land between there and the centre of town, with the sense that it had all been created especially for her and that its value enhanced her own. She was in the right setting. Here she would be what she had been unable to be before, here she would come into her own. Within a week she was dismissing her entire past life as childish and unimportant. The important thing would happen here.

She joined numerous societies and went to as many social events as she could fit into each evening. Alison, from her year ahead's superiority, mocked her. "You'll soon get tired of those cattle markets."

She knew she was beautiful, glowing with the same romantic glow that she saw in the other students' faces. Within the space of three weeks she went out with five different boys and made more friends than she had ever made in her life before. She established a niche in the library that was hers and carved delicious slices out of the freedom of the days—a lecture here, an afternoon in the library there, a meeting to form a new literary society, a meeting to defend the rights of cyclists; a conservation group, a lunch date in a pub, a concert, auditions for plays—she filled in lists of events in her university diary. It was exhilarating to read and think and write essays again, and be good at what she did. She launched into that familiar pleasure like a duck going back to water.

By the end of the third week it felt as if she'd been there half her life. In the fourth week the weather, which had been cold and autumnally crisp, suddenly relented into Indian summer, and there were three days running of intense, glowing heat. Alison emerged from her room and lay on the lawn in the sun, surrounded by heaps of books. Luxuriously abandoning her list of appointments, meetings and events, Emma joined her. The mere fact that it was possible to do so many fascinating things and meet so many fascinating people was enough, for the time being—she didn't need to be doing it.

Chapter 19

"Here," the boy said suddenly.

The lorry driver did not acknowledge him for some time. He stared ahead, slumped in his seat, left hand resting on the gear stick, right hand grasping the wheel. The juddering of the engine made the rolls of flesh on his cheeks and jowls wobble. On either side the countryside lay flat as a postcard in the garish sunlight. A green sports car overtook. "Stopping at the garage," the man said at last. He was glad the lad was getting out. Looked like a nutter. Way he held that bag—all screwed up like someone might try to grab it. And dumb as a bleeding corpse. He jerked the stick into a lower gear, and the brakes hissed and sighed. With a certain amount of satisfaction in his own skill, he pulled up with the cab door precisely opposite the door of the garage shop. The boy opened his side immediately, got out and walked away.

The driver stared for a moment, then jumped out and ran around to the front of the cab. "Don't say thanks, will yer?" The boy's back disappeared behind the garage side wall. "Bleedin' ungrateful sod." The driver went back angrily and slammed his door.

Inside the shop he bought twenty Embassy. "Just give that little bugger a lift," he complained to the woman at the till. "Not a word of thanks—nothing—just marches off." The woman jerked her head sympathetically, and made a small grimacing movement with the corners of her mouth.

At the roundabout the boy stopped, staring at a road sign. He followed the pavement round to the left in the direction of "Town Centre". The lorry driver, crawling round the roundabout, glimpsed the boy's back and hooted and made a jabbing V sign at him, but the boy did not turn his head.

Chapter 20

Emma and Alison lay on an Indian bedspread on the lawn. The sun was beating down. They both had books but neither was reading. Emma lay on her front, facing sideways towards the wall at the end of the garden. A sprawling, unpruned rose bush grew there, among the blackberry brambles and nettles. The heavy pink flowers were drooping in the sunlight; as she watched, a clump of petals suddenly dropped from one, followed by slow, individual petals fluttering after it.

She sat up and, taking up a plastic bottle from beside her book, poured a few drops of golden oil into the palm of her left hand. Slowly she rubbed it into her legs, moving her torso backwards and forwards rhythmically with each rubbing motion. "Are you going to that thing tonight?"

Alison shook her head. "I've got to get this essay done for Monday. I'd better not."

Emma sighed. "I think I'll go anyway." Slowly she lay back, her arm over her forehead to shade her eyes from the sun.

Alison sat up suddenly. "Was that the doorbell?"

Emma shrugged, and Alison got up and ran into the house. Emma strained her ears but heard nothing beyond the front door being slammed shut again. Alison must have been wrong. She watched a greenfly crawl along her wrist and start to clean itself as it came into contact with the oily part of her hand.

"It's for you!" Alison came out of the dark kitchen doorway. Behind her was a person. It looked like a boy. She did not know him. He stopped in the shaded doorway, staring out at her. The face was white, despite the heat and the parka he wore. He was holding a yellow plastic carrier bag. His sandy hair stood on end. "He said—" Alison trailed off.

Emma stared at the boy, who was staring at her. She had the sense of having seen him before. His face was not the sort of face one would recognize though. A young anonymous scruffy thug, staring at her as she scrambled to her feet in her garden. What did he want?

The hot sweat on her skin turned to ice. "Orph."

He nodded at her without smiling.

She didn't believe it. She would have given a million pounds for him to vanish into thin air. Alison stood awkwardly by the doorway. She must—"Orph. Would you like a drink?"

He nodded and she led the way back into the dark kitchen, leaving Alison outside in the sunshine. "Sit down." He sat obediently at the table, clutching his plastic carrier bag on his knees. She filled the kettle—but it was terribly cold. She was covered in goose pimples. It must be coming out of the sun so suddenly. She ran out to the lawn and got her jacket, avoiding Alison's frightened look. He was sitting in the same position. "Well, Orph. What a surprise. How are you?"

"OK."

What do you want? She couldn't think of anything else, but knew she must not say that. You can get rid of him easily, though. Just say the house is full. Say friends

103

are staying. She stared at him curiously. He had seemed so important. What a hideous, off-balance time that had been. "My missionary phase," she was calling it now, to friends. It made some funny stories, the horrors perpetrated by the kids. She was shivering. He was definitely there. He looked ill. He was dirty. The rim of the collar of his grey shirt shone with greasy dirt. His hands were grimy and one of his yellow-grey bare toes poked out of his filthy sneakers. Like something that's crawled out from underground, his pallor and dirt showed horribly strange here. Her eyes were accustomed to glossy health and well-being.

"What... Where have you come from?"

"London."

"Oh. Have you got a job there?"

He shook his head.

"Where are you living?"

"Hostel. I left." She looked at him. "There were lots of drunks. Lots of dossers."

London. A young homeless boy in London. TV documentary fodder. Dread gathered in her stomach. What do you want. "You left?" He nodded. "Have you got any money, Orph?"

He shook his head.

"How did you get here?"

"Hitched. Got a lift with a lorry up to the roundabout. Walked it from there." What do you want. She knew, of course, all along. But the horror of the prospect increased with every second. If he moved in—would they ever get rid of him? He *couldn't* move in. It would be awful—it would be ridiculous, here.

He didn't say anything. She saw he was still holding his plastic bag, and she realized suddenly that those must be his things. "Is that your clothes?"

He nodded.

Her brain was shocked into silence. All his worldly goods. In a yellow plastic carrier bag with "Wilson's

Shoes" on it. She noted how the top of the bag was wound twice around hs hand, because the slit for the handle had ripped. "I—what are you thinking of doing?" Knowing it was a cruel question.

There was a short silence. "Dunno."

The kettle was boiling. Thankfully she busied herself with cups and coffee. "Are you hung—" She bit the question back and put a loaf and butter and honey on the table. "Help yourself. I'm just taking Alison hers."

Alison jumped up when she saw her coming. "Who the hell is it? Are you all right?"

"Listen." Emma crouched on the grass, her back to the house, hand on Alison's shoulder. "Tell me what to do. He's from that kids' home where I worked."

"Has he run away?"

"No, he's allowed to leave. He's sixteen. He—he hasn't got anywhere to stay."

"He wants to stay?" Emma nodded. It was unthinkable. "Well, I suppose it's OK. There's the spare room."

"Yeah."

"But—" Alison hesitated. "What does he do?"

"Nothing."

"What's he living on?"

"Nothing."

"But Emma—what's going to happen to him?"

Emma shrugged. "Well, I suppose he'll have to stay. For a bit—unless you mind?"

"Yes, yes of course—" Alison spoke quickly, and Emma disliked her for the first time since school.

"Yes. For a bit. We'll have to sort something out." Emma stood up. "I just thought I'd better ask you."

"Yes, it's fine by me." Alison's face was unhappy.

Emma went back into the kitchen feeling morally superior. He was eating bread and honey. "Would you like to stay for a bit then?"

He nodded without looking at her.

She waited for him to thank her or look up, but he
didn't. "Well. So what've you done since you left the
home?"

"Went to London. Charing Cross. Went with this bloke
to sign on."

Sign on. Of course. "You must sign on here, mustn't
you? Tomorrow."

He nodded.

She finished her coffee. She didn't know what to say.
She had never spoken to him so much in her life before. It
was fantastic—terrible. What was going to happen? "Do
they know where you are?"

"Who?"

"The people—the hostel—the—" What a stupid
question. Nobody cared where he was. Nobody *wanted* to
know where he was. She shook her head. "There's a spare
room. I'll show you." She hesitated. "D'you want a bath?"
and didn't give him time to reply. "I've got a clean towel
in my room."

Chapter 21

The spare room contained a bed and a chest of drawers
with a mirror. The window looked over the back garden.
Next to the chest of drawers was an old fireplace, the
grate had been blocked off with hardboard. The
mantelpiece above it was narrow, embellished with a
cast-iron fleur de lys at either end. The walls and ceiling
were white, and the floor was covered in green patterned
lino.

Orph sat in the middle of the bed, his plastic bag still
clutched in his hand. Then he got up and went to the
door. There was a bolt on it, of the type that is commonly
fitted in bathrooms and toilets. He leaned against the

door to make it flush with the jamb and drew the bolt home. Then he turned the key in the lock. He put the plastic bag on top of the chest of drawers and went to the window. The back garden was overgrown and wild, it was a narrow oblong strip bordered by neighbouring houses' oblong strips. The girls had gone in, but their things were still lying on a trampled patch of grass. The window was dusty and there was a streak of dried bird shit on the lower pane. He turned and lay down on the bed, fully stretched, facing the white ceiling.

The house belonged to Emma and Alison. The air was thick with their cosy presences, their telephone calls, their endless cups of coffee. Outside the sun spilled yellow as melted butter over the sticky pears, the full-blown blowsy roses. Orph lay, white faced in his empty white room. Winter was coming. Soon the yellows and reds would go. There would be only white light and grey light, purified. Around his still room, their voices and movements murmured and lapped, tides rising and falling, but not intruding.

Chapter 22

Next morning Orph got up at ten. There was no one in the kitchen. He poured himself a cup of lukewarm tea from a teapot and ate a slice of bread and jam.

Alison appeared. "Hello." Orph nodded. "What're you doing today?" she asked brightly.

Orph swallowed his mouthful. "Gotta sign on."

"Oh, yes. D'you know where it is?"

He shook his head.

Alison laughed. "Neither do I actually. Let's have a look in the phone book." She flicked through the book a couple of times, then started to look under S. "'Social

Security: see Health and Social Security, Dept of'. Ah. H. He—" Orph watched impassively as she ran her finger up and down the columns. "Here. 'Local Social Security Offices, Pensions, National Insurance'... Is this the one, d'you think?" She looked at him hesitantly.

He shrugged.

"Well, what else could—*Un*employment? Would it be under U?" She turned the pages again. There was no entry for "Unemployment" "They don't like to make it easy for you do they? What about Employment—Department of Employment, d'you think?" More rustling of pages, then she read out triumphantly, "'Employment, Department of, ... Unemployment Benefit Offices'... That's it, isn't it?" She glanced on down the entries and checked herself. "Oh, there's a list of those Job Centre places. Are you supposed to go there first to try and find a job?"

Orph looked blank.

"When you went before—you know, those orange shops with all jobs on little postcards—?"

Orph shook his head.

She began to write an address on the back of an envelope. "It's a very long road, this—and I'm not sure which end 432 is. But anyway, it starts in the centre of town." She gave him directions and put the paper in his hand.

Orph set off in the direction Alison had indicated. The sun was shining brightly. He walked past terraces of houses similar to that he had just left, with unkempt, luxuriant gardens. The sound of a piano floated through an open window. There was little traffic. He walked through the centre of town and came to the road Alison had named. It was wide and busy, bordered with department stores and expensive furniture shops. As he went on along the street the windows of the shops became less sparkling, the goods less attractive. Second-hand gas cookers, carpet bargains tightly rolled with their knock-down prices scrawled on the underside. A DIY shop. An Indian shop, the dark window crammed with green bananas, chillies and mysterious aged cartons, their colours faded. Now the street was bordered simply by a blank wall, the shops were finished. Eventually Orph passed factory gates. There was no sign of life within. He went on.

He walked a mile and a half down the road before he reached the building. It was at the far end of another row of dingy shops. Inside it was crowded. Queues snaked around the room. There was a notice above the desk at the front of each queue: "Surnames A–D", "Surnames E–I", and so on. Orph joined the end of the A–Ds. Most people were standing in silence. A woman in a private interview booth could be heard shouting something about her husband. The windows were small and high up. A fluorescent light above the counter was flickering very fast, like blinking. Imperceptibly the queue inched forward. The man in front of him sniffed persistently and a drip trembled on the end of his bony nose, half sniffled back in on every inhalation. The people behind the desks were pale and weary, writing abstractedly or riffling through documents and letters while the claimants talked to the tops of their bowed heads. As they were finished with, most people hesitated, looking around the room as if seeking permission to leave. Then they hurried to the door, faces down, papers clutched in their hands. Orph stared at a notice on the green shiny wall. It said, "YOU ARE REQUIRED TO ATTEND THIS OFFICE AT THE TIME SHOWN ON YOUR ATTENDANCE CARD. THIS HELPS US TO GIVE YOU PERSONAL AND PROMPT ATTENTION." A telephone was ringing insistently. In the end it stopped without anyone answering it. Two lads in the M–R queue were arguing in low voices about a job. Odd words rang out loudly among the silent shuffling and sniffling. They looked around aggressively, as if to threaten anyone who listened to them.

109

When Orph got to the front he couldn't remember the address of the office where he'd signed on in London. The interviewer gave him a form to fill in and told him to go to the DHSS to claim supplementary benefit. He told him how to get there. It was another dingy concrete-slab building further down the road. Orph queued again, was interviewed again, and told to return with evidence of his address and rent. He retraced his steps into town.

Once in the centre of town, he turned off his route and wandered towards the market along the main shopping street. He walked slowly, hands in pockets, gazing unselectively around. The street was crowded, people in a hurry pushed and muttered as they were held up behind him. At the market he stepped out of the thoroughfare and stood on the cobbled corner a while staring at the seething mass of people around the stalls.

A small unsteady figure materialized from between two stalls and approached Orph familiarly. "Eh, mate! Spare a fag?" The man's face was wizened and wrinkled as an old apple, the brown skin shiny between the black creases that scored it. He moved ingratiatingly close to Orph, gesturing with a claw-like hand; skinny fingers protruded from a fingerless glove.

Orph stared at him.

"A tanner for a cup o' tea? C'mon mate, do us a favour." He bared his teeth in a grin that finished as a racking cough. His breath stank of sherry. "Do the same for you one day, eh mate, eh?"

With a violent gesture Orph pushed him away. The man's jaw dropped open and he staggered backwards, tottered and overbalanced to sprawl on the ground. Orph turned and hurried away.

The man shrieked furiously after him—"You fucker you bloody fucker fuck you—" but his abuses were quickly smothered in a spasm of coughing which kept him hunched on the ground for minutes. When he had finished he clambered cautiously up, clinging to a lamp

110

post for support. He stared in the direction Orph had gone, shaking his head. "Bloody fucker. You bloody fucker. Bloody fucker." Nobody took any notice. Still muttering, he turned and hobbled back into the market place.

Orph watched the black and white TV in the untidy sitting room from the time the children's programmes came on until close down. Emma asked him how he had got on with the social security people. She did not know what to do about the rent. After some discussion it was decided that she should type a letter stating that she was letting a room to Anthony Childs for £5 a week. "They don't need to know it's subletting. No one's going to ask. And it's not going to be for long anyway..." Who was she trying to kid? she wondered.

Chapter 23

His arrival made very little difference to the lives of Emma and Alison. If he was in he either watched TV or stayed in his room. He was never in the way. He rarely spoke. It was easy to forget he was there.

When he woke up in the mornings he lay and listened. Emma got up about eight. She wandered backwards and forwards between the bathroom and her room, sometimes she flushed the toilet two or three times. She dropped bits of cottonwool into it—Orph had seen them floating around, it was difficult to flush them away. One floorboard in the landing creaked outside her room. When she was in the kitchen she turned the radio on and arbitrary snippets of news reached Orph's ears. *A gunman today held three ... warned that if wages continue to rise ... met the president for talks ... oil prices ... fifteen killed and six ... the scale of this*

111

disaster ... an estimated two and a half million people... Emma's departure was signalled by a few moments of silence, in between the radio going off and the front door slamming behind her.

If the sun was out, it was shining full in Orph's window by now. There were cotton curtains, white with a faded floral print, the light came bleached through them. It came in slantwise from the left at about 7.30 and moved quickly over to shine full in and make a barred rectangle of white light in the middle of the floor. By 10.30 it had moved on, and the room was not directly lit. Orph lay quite still, facing the curtained window. When Emma had gone, he got up and had a piece of bread and jam, or beans if there were any. There were usually dishes in the sink from the previous night. He balanced his dirty plate and mug on top of them. No one ever asked him to wash up or cook—the other two took it in turns. They bought the food as well. He gave Emma £5 a week and at lunchtimes he bought himself pie and chips from the shop by the pub.

The house was quiet all day. Alison usually got up later, after nine. If he wasn't out, he was in his room so he didn't see her. Sometimes one of them would come back for lunch, but it was rare. They came home at four or five, sometimes with friends and bags of books with food or wine in as well. Other times they simply came back to get ready to go out again, and he ate beans again for tea.

When their friends came round they always stayed in the kitchen, clustered around the table with coffee mugs and ash trays. The room was crowded and smoky and always the debris of one meal mingled with the preparations for the next. The people who came in the evenings were all similar, aged between eighteen and twenty, dressed in clothes that were either practical or bizarre; jeans and sweater, or anything ranging from the wares of Indian stalls to drooping second-hand dresses to

112

gaudy Peruvian knitwear and pink boilersuits. There was a quality of intensity which they shared, whether it was expressed in rushed, over-articulate bursts of conversation or in drawn out silences and meaningful exhalations of smoke. There were speech rhythms and a vocabulary that they shared, full of "deadlines" and "seminars" and "tutors", a vocabulary that changed subtly over the weeks as the similar/different faces crystallized into a specific few, mainly brought home by Alison, who favoured words like "exploitation", "class structure" and "capitalism".

Alison's boyfriend was Phil, the leader of the "exploitation" crowd. He was tall, wore a large black overcoat, and introduced Newcastle Brown (which he drank from the can) into the household. He talked loudly, and said "fucking" a lot. Emma's, after she had gone through a batch none of whom lasted longer than a week, was David. He appeared infrequently. He was blonde and stocky, with broad shoulders and gold-rimmed spectacles, and maintained an ironic silence in company. He appeared older than the others and unusually well dressed in wool cloth trousers instead of jeans. He brought a bottle of whisky when he came for supper.

Orph watched television in the evenings. The only time they came in there was to watch the news or a late night film. Usually he had the front room to himself. He sat on the floor, back resting against the solid padded arm of the aged chair, much as he had sat at Mrs G.'s leaning against the sofa. Newscasters and the introducers of children's programmes and quizzes greeted him familiarly with more welcoming smiles than were ever to be seen on faces in the kitchen, and programme followed programme in scheduled order. From cartoons through to close down the civilized world unfolded itself to Orph. In domestic dramas the torridity of suburban passions were exposed; in variety shows, the legs and breasts of beautiful girls. Mid-evening cop series unleashed hygienic violence and black and white morals, while late night films wandered into the realms of soft porn and intricate murders. Occasionally rare wild animals or buildings of great historical value materialized on the screen; these were replaced at other times by monsters from outer space or newsreel of bombs falling, anthropological expeditions among little-known Himalayan villages or competitions in which people jumped over hurdles wearing outsize boots and carrying trays of eggs. The talk in the kitchen offered much less variety, and was not half so friendly.

Everyone went to bed late. If Alison's boyfriend stayed the night they made noises in her room, quite loud. Emma's didn't stay, and though they went up to her room before he went home, they didn't make any noise. On certain nights, like Saturday, they tended to be out and come in very late or not at all. Once or twice Alison and Emma coming in late together would find Orph watching the midnight movie and make a cup of cocoa for him as well and sit and giggle together around the end of the film. Excitement and the glitter of their evening encased them in a blind bubble, so that they laughed and flirted at Orph as brightly as the dancing girls on telly, and told him confidentially that the party they had been to was dreadful and pathetic.

Chapter 24

Emma was fully launched into student life, spending her days in lectures and libraries, and her evenings socializing. Most of the groups and societies she had joined seemed less interesting after a few weeks, and she abandoned them in favour of sitting in friends' rooms or their own kitchen talking. The one which she dropped most decisively after one attempt was the Cyrene soup run for tramps and derelicts.

The group gathered at 10.30 pm in a draughty wooden church hall. Sunday-school pictures of a washed-out blue Jesus suffering the little children and walking on the water decorated the bare walls. There was a motley crew of eight of them, and a harassed middle-aged man who explained what they were doing. Two girls with frizzy henna-ed hair were talking and giggling loudly about a cocktail party they'd been to. Earnest bespectacled spotty-looking boys perched on the edge of the little stage and stared at their feet, one of them kicking the side of the stage softly with his heels. Sounds echoed loudly on the bare boards. Two dim yellow electric bulbs barely lit the place. Emma felt uneasy. It was already cold and uncomfortable and peculiar, it felt very late. She wanted to go home.

They all got into the back of a van and swayed off through the dark streets. Nobody spoke. The thick scent of tomato soup was nauseating in the air. She didn't know where they were going—where did tramps stay in Leesborough? It was hard to imagine, among all this youth and optimism. The van suddenly stopped. They had hardly gone any distance. Were there some tramps already? Just around the corner? She got out, completely disorientated, half expecting a Dickensian poor house to appear before her. The street was familiar but she was so confused she couldn't remember where it was.

The driver came round. "They're usually waiting— they must be feeling lazy tonight. Here, you two, take it down to the bottom for them. Through that gate there and follow your nose. They'll be down by the hedge." He thrust a hot plastic cup and bread into Emma's hands and gave something to a boy. They stumbled away from the van into the darkness.

Emma was suddenly petrified. "Where?" she whispered.

115

"Here, it's here, I think," the boy said awkwardly. "They sleep in the churchyard, there's a bench at the end of the path." Emma's eyes adjusted to the dark as they pushed open the churchyard gate, and she suddenly noticed the floodlit church spire up, over there, magically suspended in blackness. It was cold. On either side of the path stood gravestones, casting even blacker patches of shadow across the path. She followed the boy in a panic, the mug was too hot to hold but she couldn't stop to change hands. They were well away from the road now, the traffic was growing distant. It was like being in a film, she half-expected one of the gravestones to move or split open. The grass rustled and a shadow on the path moved. Did they really sleep here? There was a little red dot of light ahead, and the murmur of a deep voice. The boy slowed down and Emma drew level with him. Behind the dot of red light, three figures took shape in the darkness. They were sitting close together. The one on the right was asleep, his head lolling back, large black nostril holes pointing at them like a gun barrel. Their bodies were dark and shapeless, she got a quick impression of macs and string, and saw that the bench was spread with newspaper. The middle one was smoking and staring at them thoughtfully. His face was thin and scored with black wrinkles, monkeyish, and he bared his teeth as he exhaled the smoke, revealing black gaps between them. He was watching them as people watch TV, sitting back, mildly curious. The one at the end was all hair and beard, his frightened eyes stared out of them like a creature disturbed in its nest. They were frozen there for a second, Emma could see herself in the tableau. Two awkward youngsters with hands outstretched; the still figures that were only half-materialized out of darkness on the bench, watching, waiting; the black shadow of the hedge behind them, the sound of cars and buses loud, from a separate world.

The boy cleared his throat. "Hello mate, would you

116

like some soup?" Emma winced, but was too embarrassed to speak herself.

"Cheers," said the middle tramp, and carefully pinching the glowing end of his cigarette between thumb and forefinger, he placed it behind his ear. His huge hand was black against the white plastic mug and hid it entirely as he closed his fist round it. It was a small amount. "Go on," he said to frightened-eyes next to him, and Emma stepped stiffly forward and held out her offerings.

The man's hand was shaking. He took the carton and looked at it then passed it back to Emma. "Open it."

She glanced quickly at the boy but he wasn't looking. She held the hot carton in her left hand and tried to peel up the stiff plastic lid with her right. It was tight and would only come off with a jerk, spilling the soup. She bent and rested it on the ground while she prized the inflexible lid off. The awful smell of the soup rose to her nostrils. "Here," she said, offering it to the man. Her voice sounded sharp. She should say something friendly. She stood up. The boy was standing awkwardly staring at the ground. "Doesn't your friend want any?" Emma asked loudly. Her voice sounded like the Queen's Speech.

"Nah!" said the middle one. "Out like a light—see— encha?" He prodded the sleeper vigorously with his elbow, and the man's arm fell off the bench armrest and dangled lifelessly by his side. Emma suddenly thought he must be dead.

"OK," said the boy abruptly. "So long." He turned and walked rapidly away.

Emma said, "Goodbye."

"Ta-ta, little lady," said the middle tramp, and winked. Emma started to run after the boy. At the bend she glanced back furtively, but they had already blended back into the blackness. Then they were back in the orange-lit street, hurrying towards the van.

"Did you find them?" asked the man.

117

"Yes, three," said the boy, and they got in and the door was slammed. The van moved off again. Emma stared at the shiny white side of the van. Nobody said anything. She visualized the two tramps' heads bent together in consuming laughter at lord and lady bountiful with their mite of soup. She hated them. Sitting there as if they owned the place, being waited on, looking down on her... She squirmed with embarrassment. Of course they would despise bearers of soup, stupid little do-gooders. But what did they know? What did they know that allowed them to sit there outside it all and be amused by people like her? The metal rim on the inside of the van cut sharply into her back as they went round a corner, and the van suddenly stopped. They were at the market.

It was desolate by night. With the empty wooden stalls casting long shadows, the market place looked twice the size it did in daylight. Noise spilled out of the van with them, the piercing voices of the girls, the harassed arranging voice of the driver, one of the spotty boys suddenly laughing out loud. They were all carrying soup and bread, ludicrous fugures straggling noisily to the fountain at the centre of the market place, where dark shapes lay and huddled on the steps, and sherry bottles glinted brownly in the light of the street lamps.

The harassed man spoke to the sprawling figures firmly. "Come on, get up, here's something to keep the cold away. Is that Derek? Come on, you old reprobate, show some life."

How they must hate him. The heaps of rags shifted and resettled their positions. The army of soup-givers advanced, with grinning and grimacing and little awkward "here you are then's" and "careful, it's hot!" Everyone fell back a step, after giving, as they do when a creature at the zoo stretches through the bars to take a morsel.

The men round the fountain grunted and snuffled and

cleared their throats, muttering "Ta, mate," and "Cheers, guv." A boy moved into the group to reach a figure on the top step, who was sitting with his back to the fountain base, crouched over something. The boy tapped his shoulder and the face jerked up furiously.

"Fuck off."

The boy moved quickly in the sudden silence.

"Who's that?" the harassed voice rang out. There was a muttered reply, and he pushed his way through to the figure on the step and pulled it to its feet. The man stood limply, his head hanging. Harassed-voice lifted the man's chin with two fingers and peered into his face. "He's not so good," he said quietly and shook the tramp by the shoulder. The man stumbled and would have fallen.

"Here!" commanded harassed-voice. The boy stepped forward uncertainly to help support the tramp. They dragged him away from the others. He was swearing continuously under his breath, softly, a stream of obscenities with no force or emphasis. "Come along, you'll be better off under cover for the night." They half-carried, half-dragged him to the van and bundled him in. The others took no notice. The pervasive soup smell spread in a cloud around them, mingling with stale alcohol. One of the boys was talking to the man called Derek. Emma walked halfway back to the van then realized they were still trying to arrange the drunk inside it, went back towards the fountain, and stopped. She didn't want to be here. At all. She stood in the shadow of a stall, afraid that one of the loud-voiced girls might speak to her. She should go. But she was frightened to walk away from them into the black shadows of the empty stalls. She might meet—what? A man who winked at her? Moved quickly by disgust she ran through the stalls and over the road. Let them think what they liked. Her heart was hammering, disgusting disgusting disgusting.

She didn't go on a soup run again, but did find herself back in the same bleak church hall for the fortnightly third world lunches, raising money for famines and natural disasters. It was much less disgusting.

Chapter 25

The girl was wearing thigh-length black boots and a short black bodice, with her large breasts bulging out of the top of it. She was sprawled on a glossy red couch, head back, eyes closed, with her legs wide apart. Another girl with nothing on at all but long black boots was kneeling on all fours, pointing between the other girl's legs, with her bare bottom exposed. She was glancing back over her shoulder at the camera with a knowing expression. Orph suddenly refocused, on a reflection in the intervening window. It was instantly recognizable— Emma. She walked past slowly. He watched her profile obscuring momentarily the bright fleshy pages on the other side of the glass. When she was past he turned and saw the reason for her slow walk. David was walking next to her. He was holding her by the arm and talking very earnestly.

Orph watched them until they were well in front of him, then began to follow. They turned left at the end of the crowded road and headed down a side street. Though the sun was shining brightly, the street was filled with shadow. It was flanked on the left by the high wall of the university grounds. There was a strange line of silver between the top of the dark wall and the blue sky. The street was nearly empty. Orph hung back and saw them turn into a gateway. He followed them through into a grassy field. There were some huge trees standing at intervals, casting wide dark shadows. In the distance, water glittered. David had his arm around Emma's shoulder and they were going towards the water. Hanging back behind trees, Orph kept them in sight. As they reached the water's edge some ducks and geese came waddling to meet them, necks outstretched greedily. He heard Emma laugh. Suddenly she turned and pretended to pummel David with her fists. He grabbed her wrists and pinned her arms to her sides, then kissed her. Their bodies moved till they were close together. Her arms went round his neck. Orph saw his hand slide down and squeeze her bottom. Their faces were pressed together. The ducks and geese lost interest and wandered away, grubbing in the shallow mud. Three of them started to glide across the pond, leaving silver trails in the water. A small twig dropped straight down from the tree Orph was standing under. At last they broke apart and moved on through the trees. When they were out of sight Orph went down to the edge of the pond. A couple of ducks moved in on him half-heartedly. He squatted at the water's edge and picked up a few stones. He aimed at the nearest duck, but missed, and it scuttled eagerly towards where the stone had plopped into the water and started sifting the water with its beak. He threw again and hit it on its side. It jabbed quickly at the hurt place with its beak, then shook itself and swam away. Soon they were all out of range. He went on throwing stones in the water until there weren't any more within reach. Then he went back towards the gate. From inside, with the sun behind him, the silver edging to the high wall was clearly visible as bits of glass. He walked slowly by it, staring up. Broken necks and pieces of bottles were set upright in the cement in a jagged line on top of the wall.

Chapter 26

Three times the unemployment office sent Orph the addresses of jobs to try for. At the third place they didn't ask him anything. The man just said, "Start tomorrow, eight o'clock." It was in a warehouse, moving crates.

That night when he went into the kitchen to get his food Phil said, "How's it going, Orph?"

So he said, "Got a job."

There was a sudden silence then everyone started talking. "That's great!" "Well done, Orph—what is it?" "Where? Hey, that's really good." He told them the name. It was quite near. "Excellent. How much pay?"

"He's the first one of us all to get a job!" said someone, amid laughter.

Phil had gone quiet. "What's the name again, Orph?" he asked. "Isn't that the place where they've been on strike for ages? Hang on." Phil ran up to Alison's room and returned brandishing a smudgily printed paper. "Here: 'Workers at Bateman's Containers, Maltby Street, move into their fourth week of strike action this Monday, in protest against low wages and filthy working conditions. Les Brown, shop steward, described the air as thick with dust from glass-fibre packing materials used to line crates and added, "people here could cough their guts up before they'd do anything about it." The men want the firm to provide proper masks and overalls, and are demanding a 16% pay rise. We'd like to bet there's no dust in managing director Andrew Smedley's office. But of course, Andrew, it *is* only the workers whose health is suffering. And they're easy to replace, aren't they?'" Phil threw the paper down dramatically. "You can't go there, Orph!" Orph gazed at him. "But I don't see how in hell they can be recruiting new people, if everyone's on strike. Did you see anyone working there, Orph?"

Orph nodded, the centre of attention. "I saw about five or six men, moving crates."

"And wasn't there a picket? Some people outside, telling you not to go in?"

Orph shook his head.

"Jesus Christ," exclaimed Phil, "I'm going to ring Harry. It's all right—I'll eat later." He vanished, leaving a concerned conversation bubbling over the injustices perpetrated by capitalists and the types of ailments which could be caused by dust in the lungs.

Emma perched herself next to Orph. "You mustn't go, you know," she said quietly. "That's really dangerous. Phil will tell you what to do—you'll have to go and tell them at the labour exchange I suppose. Do they stop your money if you don't go?"

Orph didn't know. They all wanted to know exactly what he had seen in the warehouse. Were there clouds of dust? And were the men coughing? Were the crates heavy? What exactly did they have to do?

Phil returned full of gratitude from the man called Harry; he hadn't known the firm were recruiting new workers on the sly—now the union could really go to town on them. "The bastards! Bloody barefaced cheek— incredible, isn't it?"

The conversation frothed with indignation. Later that evening Phil reassured Orph that he should certainly not worry about the job. "Just don't turn up. The people who do are likely to get a black eye for their troubles anyway—they'll put on a big picket tomorrow." Orph nodded, his face expressionless. "Hey Orph, I've just thought. Will they stop your money?"

Orph didn't know.

"Shit. Look, if they do—here's a couple of quid—it's all I've got on me. Let me know, OK?"

123

From then onwards Phil talked to him quite regularly. "Tell me where else they send you, OK? I bet they're all places like that. Have they sent you to that scrap yard yet? Ross and Watson's?" Orph hadn't heard of it. "Well, don't touch it with a barge pole. Don't go near the fucking place. D'you know what happened there last year? A bloke was killed. They were piling up the cars with a crane—him standing at the bottom directing things, waving his arms about—car slips off the top of the pile and scrunch—flattened!" Little flecks of spittle gathered at the corners of Phil's mouth when he got excited, and he often patted Orph on the shoulder when he talked to him.

One day he brought him a bright red jumper. "My mum knitted it. It's a bit small. I thought it might fit you."

Emma watched as he tried it on. "It looks very nice," she said. "Thanks, Phil." As if he had given it to her. Phil always said hello and goodbye to him now.

Chapter 27

November. It was dark early in the evenings now. By four o'clock the darkness was gathering, and the lighting of street-lamps made it night. For several days running, a cold mist which only hovered over streams and ponds in daylight, thickened with the darkness into a fog which flowed silently along streets, between houses, over cars.

One afternoon Orph left the house as it was getting dark. The fog lay wet and cold across the street and coagulated in heavy drops on his skin and hair. It muffled his footsteps and quickly absorbed the strength of street-lights, so that they twinkled as vaguely and ineffectually as stars, casting no light. Cars appeared with no warning, glowing at the last minute like ghosts. He walked apparently aimlessly, turning corners at random. The few people he passed were there then gone again in an instant, without the forewarning of footsteps. He passed a cluster of little local shops, butcher, post office and newsagent, invitingly cosy and lighted with Christmas fairy lights framing the windows. People paused in the lit doorways, unwilling to launch themselves into the blackness again, and a group of children stood outside the newsagent counting out sweets. Orph glanced casually through the post office window, then moved a few houses down the street and positioned himself in a gateway.

The children came straggling past, abruptly audible, then as abruptly silenced. "—said you'd give me two for a gobstopper. It's not fair."

"I never, I don't even want your smelly gobstopper anyway, I'd rather've had chews—" Orph stood invisibly, watching their black shapes pass, and then the silence. After a few minutes another small figure materialized, slow-moving this time. It was thick and shapeless, the blob of its head curiously broadened by some sort of hat. The hunched outline of the back and blob head gave it the look of a tortoise—the tortoise Orph had spotted at the post office counter, minutes ago. As she shuffled past, Orph moved silently out on to the pavement behind her. She was going very slowly and making a slight whistling sound through her teeth each time she breathed out. He walked close enough to hear her. From behind, the bulk of her silhouette was rendered even broader by the fat, shiny handbag she clutched to her right side.

The little whistling figure and her silent shadow moved on away from the shops and turned left at the first corner. When they had passed the third ineffectual haloed streetlamp Orph took a quick step to bring himself level with her, and snatched at the bag—pulling it backwards from under her encircling arm. It should have come away easily, but it didn't. If he had paused to watch her finish her business through the post office window, he would have seen that after she had stashed her pension away she had wound the long shoulder strap of the bag twice around her bony wrist before tucking it under her arm, with the careful deliberation of an old person performing a movement ritualized by habit.

It slid from under her arm, but remained attached to her. She gave an astonished squawk, and Orph pulled violently at the bag again, unbalancing her. She toppled towards him, black mouth wide open but making no sound. Falling, she pulled the bag from his grasp. In the muffling, deadening air she crashed horribly loudly, her rounded shape disintegrating into a black mass on the pavement. Orph grabbed again at the gleam of the shiny leather bag and again her puppet arm tugged out with it.

He was breathing harshly and whispering now on his breaths—"Let go fuck you stupid fucking cow let go let fucking go—" He threshed the bag from side to side and the attached arm danced in the dark air beneath it. The old lady was making a noise like a saw, not panting or sobbing or screaming, but sawing harshly and desperately with her open black mouth and open white staring eyes. He kicked at her noisy staring head and felt along the strap to her papery hand. The strap was tight across her knuckles, twisted and pulled tighter by his tugging at it. Swiftly he unwound it and the limp arm dropped back into the shapeless blackness of the rest of her. Orph vanished, and the sounds of the struggle, of movement and harsh breathing, ceased abruptly. Filling up space, the dark mist closed in over the black lump on the pavement.

Chapter 28

Emma's relationship with David followed a predictable course. She had already decided that she was far too old to still be a virgin.

That's it then. Red and raw. Sore and raw. Does he think I—was it all right then?

She knew it wasn't. The desire that had made her skin prickle with sensitivity switched off, click, when he tried to do that. And there was a dry tight body not knowing what it should do, and a feeling of turning a knife while she shrank back horrified to feel herself wounded. Is that what it is? Can he tell? She didn't know. Smile. Get dressed. Kiss. Is he looking at me? I can't tell. I don't know what it should be. It's happened, then.

He stands there in the light, in the doorway. Thinking what?

"Why don't you stay? It's crazy to go home now."

Again. Why don't I stay? "No—I just want to. It's OK." Dry peck on the cheek again I'm cold I'm shivering what's the time? Unlock the bike in the dark and the chain's stuck in the spokes clanking and clattering, cold numb fingers weave it through here—here—sod it. She pulled hard and the chain flew out of the spokes and hit her knuckles. Slow down. Front light. Back light. Bag strap over head, crossing the chest. Gloves? In his room still, no, I'm not going back. He's still standing there, it's taking so long. OK. She negotiated the clumsy bike out of the gateway, backwards, keeping the gate open by bumping it gently with her hip, turned the front wheel now and was out. "Goodnight."

"Emma?" She waited, blank, for him to say something. He took a step forward, she couldn't see his face because of the light behind him. "Nothing. Goodnight."

What should I say? Slowly, clumsily, she got on to the bike and the shock of pain as she sat on the saddle brought it back to her. I've done it. We did it. She stood on the pedals and rode home slowly, crouching over the handlebars, not wanting to sit. Blackness everywhere, each light looked alone and helpless, shining away to no effect, the blackness was everywhere. Few cars, no one about. Red eye of traffic light. She straightened her back, feet on the ground, waiting. Amber. Green. She stood over the bike, eyes fixed on the light. Nothing happened. Amber. Red. She hadn't gone. What was it? She was standing there in the empty dark with a bicycle, and a light was telling her what to do. Amber. Green. Go now. It stared at her, imploring her. Go now. But her muscles were petrified. She stared at the green eye, waiting for the message and command to filter through her brain. Nothing. I'll stand here all night. Amber. Red. Minutes are ticking by. No traffic. It tells you all night, on and on and on—go—wait—stop—go—wait—stop. Even when no one's here to see it, messaging to no one. Go. Stop. A car was speeding up from behind. Red/amber changed to green. The driver shifted gear and sped on without stopping. Look how easily he got through. No problem. Didn't even stop to think. Amber. Red. If I wait till it's green again. How can I make myself go? Amber. Now. Green. Her brain lifted her right foot on to the pedal and pushed the left toes against the ground. Her fingers tightened on the handgrips. Very slowly the bike began to move. She wobbled, nearly sat down then remembered, pushed the left pedal down hard and was moving. In the middle. Amber. What if I stopped here? In the middle. Amber red. Just stood here. Nothing. Nothing would happen because I'm not really here. It gives its message and I don't go. I'm not really here at all.

Slowly, incredibly slowly, the bike wobbled across the controlled square of road. Her fingers were clenched

128

tight on the grips, painfully cold, stiffening. Coming up now. Street light. Bushes. Not ride on the gravel tonight. Not balance. Every movement was an old woman's, as she dismounted slowly, carefully, whose is this body? What's it done? and carefully pushed the bicycle into the drive into the dark shadow of the bushes and the gravel crunched under her feet and the tyres now it's very dark. Afraid of those bushes? You were once. What a good hiding place. But there's no one there. There's no one there and who cares if there is, no one will harm me. I'm not here either. Her fingers unclasped from the handlebars slowly, one at a time, like prising open a box, and she held them cold and immovable in front of her. What? The stars are shining. I don't care. Where's the chain? But her fingers couldn't bend and fiddle the chain through the spokes, they were clumsy and aching with cold. She stood, helpless a moment by the wall with the icy chain in her hand. What must I do? Get the key. Unlock the door. Go in.

She couldn't. The chain dropped, and she crouched to find it, clasping her hands down between her legs for warmth. And began, slowly and hopelessly, to cry. She was this—a small thing by the wall in the dark, unable to lock her bicycle. Different, not transformed—nothing. She had no will, she had no feeling. Not to say, "I feel that", or to want to stay or to want to move. Not to know that it had been important—to know that it hadn't. This happens to everybody. But it's different. I can never move now. I'm here, my hands are cold, the chain's in the gravel. There's no warmth in me.

Pins and needles started in her foot and she shifted to ease it and toppled over, and was shocked enough to scramble up. Blindly, the unwilled tears streaming which were nothing to do with her, she went to the door and forced the foreign hands to open the purse and identify the key and press it into the stubborn lock and twist it.

129

She went in. They must all be in bed. It's dark here too, with orange patterns on the floor from the street-light falling in. This is where I live. So why am I crying? Why didn't I stay? I just didn't. She undressed in the dark and got into bed, icy cold, and lay obediently under the blankets waiting for something to happen, for some warmth to come back, for her eyes to stop pouring and pouring these tears that were nothing to do with her. I've done it. I'm different now. But she felt she would never be different, though she wanted that more than anything in the world.

Chapter 29

When Emma got home at 5 pm the next day there was no one in. The house was a mess. Last night's dishes were piled high in the sink, the table was smeared with breadcrumbs and cigarette ash. She felt empty. She made herself a cup of tea and sat at the table without bothering to wipe a clear patch. Where was Alison? With Phil? At a meeting? And where was Orph? She couldn't imagine. Suddenly she thought he might be in his room, and went upstairs. She stood holding her breath outside his door, listening. No sound. "Orph?"

No reply. Gently she tried the handle. The room stank. She crossed quickly to the window and drew back the curtains. She had a struggle to open the window. One of the sash cords was broken, and it obviously hadn't been opened for years. She managed to raise it a couple of inches, and breathed in deeply. She turned to examine the room. His bed was like an animal's, a nest of dirty blankets and sheets. They were wound round into a knot in the middle of the mattress, leaving the edges bare. There were some neatly folded, dirty clothes on the chest of drawers. She walked around the space, looking at it. Dust had gathered in balls along by the skirting board. A row of cigarette butts stood like soldiers on the mantlepiece, balancing ash. There was no fire. That had not occurred to her before. She and Alison had electric fires in their rooms. She would have to do something, take him to the laundrette, and show him how to use a vacuum cleaner.

She realized that she was staring at something under the bed. Something ridged. There were stacks of magazines there. Great piles of them, with thick spines and glossy covers. It was strange, she couldn't recognize the shape of them. *National Geographical* or something, must have been left by the people before. She pulled one out. Glossy, thick, pink flesh leapt to her eyes. *Playboy*. A spread-eagled naked woman, hands fondling breasts, wearing a bright red smile. Emma's eyes blurred. She went quickly to the stairs and ran down to place a kitchen chair near the front door, so that it would bang if he came in. She pulled out all the magazines. Pornography! There were stacks of them, fifteen or twenty at least. Incredulous, she leafed through the pile. *Bondage, Mates, Playboy...*

Naked girls ogled her from the shiny covers. A large blonde, half reclining on a black sheeted bed holding herself open between the legs. Emma sat back on her heels. Where had they come from? Why had he got them? She opened one—a photostory of two girls who invite the electrician in—and stared at the poses and pouts and proffered nipples and cunts. The women smiled out with plastic faces, not human beings but dolls for one purpose. Imagine them doing it, manipulating their cunts for the camera, legs round the tripod, face aching with smiling. On the next page was a lot of print—a story about a girl who went motorbike riding naked with her boyfriend at night and achieved multiple orgasms by driving over fields. A letter from a man describing the seduction of his

131

best friend's wife: "She was saying 'No, no,' over and over again, but she was hot and wet for it, her quim was brimming with juice."

Emma stared at the words. She stood slowly and went to the window. She was hot. Incredulously, she realized that she was sexually aroused. A wave of hotness went over her, a kind of thickness in her mind. She could feel her nipples pricking against her shirt. She held herself perfectly still. No. I don't believe it. Hotness came up and up in her, and her knees were suddenly weak. She moved stiffly forward and gently pressed her groin against the window ledge in front of her. Sharp pleasure and expectation lit up through her belly and breasts and she turned quickly back to the wall, beside the window so that she could not be seen, and slid her hand inside her jeans. Suddenly she was standing there gasping for breath, shaking, her right hand held in front of her as if it belonged to someone else. She slid to a sitting position, back against the wall. She felt sick. The hot desire shrivelled into nausea. She could feel what seemed like a strong pulse beating inside her, between her legs, and she squeezed them together to drown it away. Her stomach was nauseated. Like an animal—because of that—those pictures. She didn't want to believe her own reaction. Slowly she raised her hand to her nose and smelt the smell of herself. She was shaken by disgust.

She crawled over to the magazines again and mechanically turned the pages. Body after body, breast after breast, cunt after cunt. Shiny, impersonal, disgusting, degrading. How could she—could anyone? And yet she had felt like that.

Quickly she piled them up and pushed them back under the bed. Stood, then knelt again to check that they were as she'd found them. The room looked the same? Closed the curtains, shut the door, moved the chair from the front door. She went and washed her hands carefully, as if they were contaminated, and went back to her room.

132

She imagined him leafing through and pausing to stare at a particular page. No. But why not? What had she thought he was? He had needs and lusts, the same as anyone else. A body, the same as anyone else. I bet he's never even touched a girl, she thought. The enormity of his life rushed at her. What did he do? She began to cry in guilt and self-pity. He had turned into a man who read pornography. Disgusting, degrading. But who did he have? What were his pleasures? And I did that. I am the same too.

But his mysterious life became something tangible and stinking. What had she expected? His life must be full of disgusting incidents. Suddenly she thought, I will never be able to get rid of him. He'll follow me through my life like a disease, something dirty I don't understand that clings to me. How will I ever get rid of him? When I leave here, wherever I go he'll come after me, move into my house— She wished violently that she had never invited him. It wasn't fair. But I. The other little voice piping up, trying to get through. But I. Remember?

As time went by, Emma pushed this incident completely out of her mind. But Orph retained, for her, an extra aura of ugliness now—something that made her shrink from contact with him and avoid his eyes. He made her guilty. Later still, an image came to her of their lives, with the remorseless momentum and helplessness of a nightmare. As if they were on railway tracks, Orph and she, rolling silently near to each other, tracks crossing but never touching. Sliding on to different ends, in places far apart. She could not speak to him as, in a dream, your muscles turn to water and you cannot stir to save your life. She could do nothing but stand and watch, paralysed. His life is his own. I am not responsible.

When she and David were coming back from town with some shopping, she saw him. He was staring at her

133

across the street, and she recognized him with a cold jolt. Too late, she smiled and nodded. She didn't say anything to David, but she glanced back over her shoulder twice on the way home, and although she didn't see him, she was sure he was still there.

Several days later David suddenly said, "That boy of yours—the lout—is he all right?"

"What do you mean?"

"Is he all right in the head?"

"What do you mean?" She was filled with dread.

"I keep seeing him. Everywhere. In town. Going home. On my way here. He's always hanging about, staring at me."

Emma re-experienced the cold shock of meeting those dead eyes across the street. "I—it's just coincidence. He's unemployed, remember, he spends most of the day wandering about."

"You should make him get a job. He's peculiar. I don't like the idea of him hanging around you all the time. You'll wake up one morning to find your house stripped clean. You're asking for it."

"Leave him alone." She was angry. David's matter-of-factness was crass. She knew Orph watched them. There was nothing she could do. Superstitiously she dreaded making something unthinkable happen by talking about it. If it was unspoken, it was at least partly not there.

Chapter 30

One night they were sitting on the sofa watching TV when Orph came in. They moved quickly when the door opened, and Emma said, "Hello!" very brightly. Orph slumped on the floor, leaning against the sofa arm as he always did. There was some politician on the screen. It was very quiet after Orph had settled down, and the man's voice seemed unnaturally loud. "Of course, we view the prospect of increasing unemployment with alarm," he was saying in a slurred oily voice, "but we are totally unwilling to throw away the sacrifices already made—already *made*—" he stressed as the interviewer tried to interrupt him, "by vast sections of the working population of this country, in terms of real income, for what can only be a temporary..."

Emma and David were moving on the sofa. Orph heard the very faint sound of a breathed whisper from David, and Emma whispering back, "No!" Then there was a gentle brushing sound, as of skin touching skin repeatedly. A slight shift of position on the sofa—it moved fractionally, behind his back—and more whispers. On TV the politician continued to propound his views on what could be done for the young and discontented unemployed. Emma seemed to sigh—he could hear her breathing, regularly but slightly fast; they seemed to be squirming about as if not quite comfortable.

Suddenly she asked, "Where've you been, Orph? Somewhere interesting?"

There was dead silence before he answered. "No. Just out."

Then furtive movements again, the slight rustling of cloth and skin. David was whispering again, but the words weren't clear. Then he changed to talking aloud. "Well in that case, I'll be off." There was a lot of rustling and movement.

"David—" she said, she was half-laughing.

"Yes?" He sounded very polite. The sofa rocked a little as he stood up.

"Hang on!" As he went out of the door she ran after him, pulling the door to carelessly after her. Orph sat still, the politician continued to talk. They were kissing in the hall, he could hear the wetness of their mouths and the rustling of their bodies pressing against each other. Then Emma whispering. They giggled. Instead of the front door opening, they went upstairs, and the bedroom door closed firmly behind them.

Orph was sitting in the same position, but a different programme—a comedy—was on when they came downstairs. David waited in the hall. Emma opened the door into the kitchen and spoke to Alison.

Her voice carried clearly. "We're going over to David's, in case you wonder where I am. Listen, will you be here for supper tomorrow? I was planning to cook something nice. And what about Phil? OK—see you—" The kitchen door closed, then the front door opened and closed, and their footsteps vanished into the night.

After five more minutes, Orph got up and switched off the TV, reducing the jolly couple on the screen to a small persistent white dot. Moving silently, he went up the stairs, not to his own room but to Emma's. He went in and locked the door quietly behind him. When his eyes were accustomed to the dark, he crossed to the window and opened the curtains so the street-lamp shone in. He moved around slowly, looking at the books and records and plants, standing still to stare at the array of postcards stuck on a long strip of black paper. Kneeling down in front of the chest of drawers, he opened the bottom one silently and put his hand in to touch the clothes. He picked garments out one by one and examined them closely. A T-shirt, a bra, a pair of tights. Then he closed the drawer slowly and went to the bed. The yellow and red Indian bedspread was rumpled. He laid his hand on it but lifted it away again quickly as if he had been burned. The house was very quiet. Silently he took off his clothes. Shirt then pumps then trousers and pants, till he was standing skinny and orange-palely lit, naked by the window. He pulled the bedcovers right back and knelt over the bed, burying his face in the

136

sheets. Like a mole or some blind creature he rubbed his face up and down the sheet, nuzzling and sniffing, eyes closed, neck outstretched. Then he reached down and pulled the blankets up over himself. For a while he lay quite still, face down, buried in the pillow. Then he turned on to his side and taking the pillow in his arms, hugged it to himself, lying with his eyes wide open staring into the darkness.

He stayed there until Alison had gone out next morning. When he was dressed he gently remade the bed, stroking the pillow before he pulled the sheet up over it, pausing to brush the bedspread with his fingertips before leaving the room.

Chapter 31

One day when it was pouring with rain Orph was sent to Haltons, a small textile firm in the industrial part of town. There were two people standing outside the gates in the rain. As he turned into the gateway one of them waved a sodden piece of paper under his nose. Orph sidestepped and it fell to the ground.

The other man suddenly leapt forward. "Orph! Christ Almighty, have they sent you here?" It was Phil. He was wearing a knee-length grey plastic mac and Christopher Robin hat, and his pockets were stuffed with wet leaflets upon which the print had already run so severely that they were practically illegible. "You don't wanta go in," Phil gabbled excitedly. "Don't touch it with a barge pole. They are real wankers, I'll tell you."

Orph stood in the middle of the pavement, his hands in his pockets, the rain running through his short hair and down his unblinking face.

"Listen, I'll show you—" Phil peered up and down the

street, then asked the other man what the time was. Ten to nine. "Oh, bugger it then, it'll do for today. Most of 'em are in, aren't they?"

"Ay. Most of 'em are in." The man smiled sourly. "See you." He shook himself and walked off rapidly.

Phil grabbed Orph's elbow. "Let's go and have a cup of tea and I'll tell you—" He led the way up the street and round the corner to a dingy little transport café, taking his mac off and shaking it vigorously in the doorway before entering. The woman at the counter seemed to know him. He bought two cups of tea and two buns and ushered Orph to a table beside the mucky window. "OK? Jesus, you're even wetter than me!" He took a big slurp from his cup. "What'd they sent you for?"

Orph shrugged. "Sweeping up, I think."

Phil nodded. "See that bloke? The guy who was at the gate? They sacked him two weeks ago. And now they've got someone else doing his job for £11 less! Of course, they're pretending it's not the same job." He shook his head and leaned back in his chair. "It's like the bloody dark ages. And none of the others gives a toss. Got these printed—oh shit—" He dug in the mac pockets and pulled out the wet scrumpled leaflets. "We've been standing there for the past two mornings as they've been going in to work—they don't even read 'em. I'm all right Jack, that's all they can think, they just look the other way until something actually threatens the crust that's going into their own mouths. Here, that's yours." He pushed one of the buns towards Orph. "Talk about solidarity. It's a fucking joke. Mind you—" he hesitated, "I get the impression that Mike isn't the most popular of men, which doesn't help, you know. I mean, if it was everybody's bosom buddy, there might be more reaction. He's a funny bloke—too quiet, like he's judging you all the time. Even so, if they can get away with it with him—" Phil gulped at the rest of his tea and twisted round towards the counter. "What's the time, luv?"

138

"Ten past nine."

"Shit, I've got a meeting at nine thirty. Which way you going? Into town?" He led the way out into the rain again. "See you, kid. You wanna get a hat—this stuff'll erode your brain!" Orph watched him disappear at a half-run around the corner.

That night they were all at the house. It was still raining, the house was full of wet clothes and damp bodies, the close smell of drying hair. Orph lay on the floor in the living room watching TV while the others sat and talked over the remains of supper. At five to ten Alison announced that she wanted to watch the news and everyone came into the sitting room. As the last stroke of Big Ben vibrated in the air, the picture moved jerkily around a large farmhouse, where at one point a head was visible at an upstairs window. *A gunman today held two people hostage in a farmhouse in Dorset.* The picture changed. *A civilian was killed, and a soldier wounded in Ulster...* The pictures continued to change, accompanied by the sharp dramatic voice.

Halfway through Phil suddenly leaned forward and turned the set off. There was a shocked silence.

"What are you doing?" said Alison.

"You know what it's going to say. It's always the bloody same. Wars here. Riots there. Unemployment rising. A new nuclear reactor. And a natural disaster thrown in for good measure. What's the point?"

Alison rose and switched on the set again.—*two thousand refugees who have made their camp near the bridge where fighting still rages, despite the peace initiative made by the rebels...*

"See?"

"I like to know what's going on," said Alison.

"Do you? Do you?" Phil sat up. "And do you think they'd tell you the half of it?" He was prickling for a fight.

139

"Well, they probably tell you more than you'd learn with the set switched off."

"Lies, that's all it is, lies and propaganda." Phil sank back into his chair, muttering. Everyone ignored him. "What d'you think, Orph? You must watch enough."

Orph did not turn his unblinking gaze from the screen. "Load of rubbish."

"Hah, hah!" Phil leapt forward, slapping his thighs in delight. "Load of rubbish! See! See! Load of rubbish!"

"Ssshh," said Emma irritably.

"Load of rubbish, load of rubbish," chanted Phil.

Alison turned round. "Piss off. Go in the kitchen and wait till the news is finished. I want to listen."

"Yes madam, certainly madam, anything you say." He rose, tugging at his forelock. "Far be it from me, madam, to intrude when great minds are improving themselves." He disappeared into the kitchen and shut the door. When the news ended a comedy programme came on. Everyone sat watching it, except for Alison who glanced at the kitchen door. After a few minutes she rose quietly and went into the kitchen. Phil was sitting at the table. He had pushed all the dirty dishes up to one end and had the *Guardian* spread out in front of him. To his left were several strips of cut-out paper.

"What're you doing?"

"Reading the news."

"But you're cutting things out."

"Yup. I'm making you a little tapestry of meaningful news items." She moved to see the cut-out paper strips. They were headlines.

HOPES RISE FOR IRAN HOSTAGES

OIL PRICES RISE

CEGB PLANNING FOR EXPANSION OF NUCLEAR POWER

GOVERNMENT PLAN TO CUT DOLE LINK WITH PRICES

FRESH FIRE ATTACKS ON WELSH HOLIDAY HOMES

KAMPUCHEA DENIES BRUTALITY CHARGES

OECD OPTIMISTIC ON FUTURE OF THE WORLD
POOR TO DEMAND MORE HELP

He laid another beneath the last one:

SUGAR PRICES FACE A CRUCIAL WEEK

"Good, isn't it?" He was looking pleased. "Makes a lot of sense, doesn't it?"

Alison laughed. "I like it. It's a poem. Let's stick them up. Put this one on top." She pointed to OECD OPTIMISTIC ON FUTURE OF THE WORLD. She fetched paper and sellotape and they stuck the finished sheet to the kitchen wall.

Emma wrinkled her face disapprovingly when she read it. "It's pretentious."

"Oh hoity toit," said Phil. "Listen to Lady Muck."

"It is. It's stupid. It's just the sort of thing a load of students would have on the wall."

"Well, you *are* a load of students."

"That's the point. There's no need to play up to it."

Phil pranced about the room, holding his nose. "Ahy'm note a styudent! Nyah nyah nyah!" Suddenly he put his face close to Emma's. "I'm gonna bring you some posters and stick them up. Real studenty ones. Pictures of Marx and Chairman Mao. Quotations by Che Guevara. Ho ho!" He and Alison danced off, leaving Emma with the dishes and the "poem" on the wall.

Over the following week Phil and Alison added to their poem, sticking up a new sheet of paper alongside the first. Emma read it and refrained from comment. Orph also read it without commenting. Alison was so delighted by it that she started buying other newspapers, in the hopes of discovering a real gem. On Tuesday they added:

BOMB BLASTS AIRLINE OFFICES
SIXTEEN TERROR ACT DETAINEES FREED
DUPLICATE MURDER BY IRA

141

MORE CUTS PLANNED IN PUBLIC HOUSING

NURSE "BRUISED" IN POLICE CUSTODY

AUGUSTUS JOHN PAPERS FETCH £57,000 AT SOTHEBY'S

The weather suddenly turned very cold. It was building up to Christmas. On Wednesday the snow fell. It came in flurries, with a strong wind, and drifted so that the landscape became lop-sided. The wire-netting fence separating their garden from the one to the right became three-dimensional. Instead of settling on top of the strands of wire, the clinging snowflakes were blown sideways by the wind and fixed there by night frost. The fence had a solid white shadow. The temperature continued to drop, and all the tyre marks and footprints casually made in the snow were immortalized in ice. Icicles hung at a strange angle from branches and guttering, deflected from gravity by the wind.

Alison and Emma were getting ready to go home for Christmas. Orph went into the empty kitchen and read the new headlines.

THATCHER WARNS THE WEST AGAINST MARXISM

WINDSCALE FITTER WAS CONTAMINATED
IN NUCLEAR PLANT

CARLISLE SPARES THE LIFE OF QUANGO

MURDER OF DISCO GIRL—MAUREEN DUMPED UNDER
HOLLY BUSH

(Someone had scrawled after this one, "Seasonal".)

MARRIAGE AND DIVORCE UP AND UP

GLOOM ON JOBLESS

Below was a small boxed item cut from the *Sun*. Alison had put a large exclamation mark above it:

BEAT THE FESTIVE FATTIE TRAPS!

Want to indulge in all the Christmas goodies without wrecking your keep-slim-plan? MAKE LOVE! Make love at least once a day next week! One after-lunch cuddle is worth 10 DATES (the edible kind), 3 CHOCOLATE LIQUEURS, or a PINT OF BITTER!

142

Orph made himself a cup of tea. Then he went up to his room. Last night's condensation had frozen in opaque patterns on the inside of his window. He laid his hand against the ice and held it till a dribble of water ran down his wrist. Then he looked out through the blurry little window at the bright white world outside. Next day, although the whole window was frozen over, the shape of a hand was clearly visible among the ice patterns.

Alison and Emma discussed Orph on the landing.

"It would be stupid. He can't possibly come home with me." Emma was aggressively definite.

"It's not for long anyway," said Alison. "I'll be back in six days."

"The length of time isn't the point really is it?"

"No."

"What about Phil?"

"What about Phil?"

"Will he be here over Christmas?"

Alison considered. "He might be. Yes, I think he will. I'll ask him—he could keep an eye on him, cook him a meal or something."

"Yes. Oh yes, if he would." They were both relieved.

Emma was the last to leave. Orph sat in his room and listened to the rustles and bangs and repeated hurried footsteps on the stairs. There was a period of silence, then a knock at his door.

She opened it and put her head round. "I'm off now, Orph—so long. I'll see you in a week or so. You know where to find Phil if you need anything, don't you?"

He nodded.

"Well, goodbye then. Happy Christmas!" She ran downstairs and the front door slammed hard. Orph sat on his bed, feet resting squarely on the floor, his elbows on his knees. The stairs creaked, once, twice, like a complaint cut short. Outside, there was a sudden flurry of noise as a group of starlings squabbled over the stale contents of the breadbin, cleaned out by Alison. The birds shrieked and flapped then took their argument further away down the garden. A deeper silence descended. The water tank had been gurgling all morning, refilling itself. Now suddenly it stopped hissing and plunking. Slowly Orph stood up, head cocked on one side as if listening. He walked silently to his door, opened it, and stood still in the doorway. A car went past. There was a sudden persistent humming noise. Orph walked in the direction of the sound, towards the kitchen. As he opened the kitchen door the humming ceased. Silence. A blackbird tin-can-clattered alarm outside. Everything was turned off—the gas fire, the light, all the plugs except the fridge. The table had been hastily wiped, there were smears on the grey formica surface and a fine trail of crumbs. The draining board was piled high with newly washed plates and saucepans balanced on top of each other. Someone had wiped around the sink too and left just their own breakfast dishes in the bowl. Orph went to the window and smeared a clean patch in the condensation. Snow, a shroud covering everything. He shivered. Picking up the box of matches from on top of the cooker, carefully, so they didn't rattle, he went over to the gas fire and squatted beside it. He struck a match and lit the fire, turning up the controls to high. The fire hissed loudly, like an indrawn breath going on impossibly long. Suddenly the humming began again. Orph went to the fridge and opened the door. The sound stopped. He shut the door. The sound began again, blotting out the noise of birds, of the fire. He pulled out the fridge plug. The noise stopped.

Orph did not go out at all that day. He wandered around the house, in and out of every room, opening doors, looking in cupboards, rifling through drawers. Carefully replacing things as he found them. Moving slowly and quietly, as if someone might hear him and be angered by

144

his presence. For lunch he had a cold tin of baked beans and a slice of bread and butter. The look of the table changed. No longer hurriedly smeared clear. Now there was an empty jagged-topped tin, a half loaf surrounded by crumbs, a newly opened damp half pound of butter from the defrosting fridge. A dirty tin opener, a spoon and the bread knife. Orph sat back and looked at these objects. Then he went and switched on the TV.

He watched a lot of TV over the following days. Every now and then he would switch off the set and sit completely still, in the attitude of a person listening. After a while he would switch it on again. The switchings on and off did not coincide with any timings that had ever entered a programme planner's mind. Orph did not watch television in programmes. He turned it on and off like a tap, and it spewed forth a variety of Christmas images. An ecstatic family in party hats crouched over the latest board game. A distressed-looking man staring helplessly at a huge Christmas pudding, while a woman in the foreground smiled knowingly and tapped a bottle of indigestion pills. A dance group in corsets and suspenders, eyes made up like wounds, moving around and over each other very slowly, staring provocatively at the camera. The exploded remains of a van presumed to have contained a home-made bomb in Northern Ireland. Two plump smiling men leaning far back in deep swivel chairs, exchanging witticisms, basking in the approval of their audience. A news reader with huge bags under his eyes. Father Christmas in a children's ward, trying to smile through his beard. A man with pointed ears on another planet fingering a small dead furry thing and shaking his head ruefully. Little boys in long dresses raising their throats as one and emitting clear song. People singing. In chorus lines, churches, sitting rooms, army barracks. A group of soldiers raising pint pots to the camera. Sudden explosions of snowflake-stars dancing across the screen

145

to form words—*For The Best in Christmas Entertainment...* A laconic singer whose fellow artistes were all besieged and shot during the course of their song, jumping up to rapturous applause. Carpet bargains hurry hurry hurry roads blocked by snow a woman laughing the Christmas tree in Trafalgar Square a child blinded by gunshot I'm dreaming of a white the Pope bisto for a rich say it with flowers the Ripper strikes again police chief accused of corruption a film star dancing in the snow shampoo to bring your hair to life an old woman wrapped in a blanket by a switched-off fire don't be vague ask bang bang.

Orph watched and listened with no sign of reaction, except that now and then he would rise, switch it off, and stand listening.

Over the days the house changed. Whenever he moved or used anything in the kitchen or sitting room, he left it where he'd used it. From the original bean can and half-loaf, the following collection built up on the kitchen table: a butter wrapper, a half packet of biscuits, an open jar of Nescafé, an open 2lb sugar bag, the silver wrappings of four Kraft cheese-spread triangles, two more bean cans, two tomato soup cans, an empty milk bottle, a Spam tin, a half-eaten tin of creamed rice pudding, six cups containing various dregs, and numerous plates and items of cutlery. On the floor in front of the TV were two more biscuit packets, the cellophane wrapper of a pound of mild English cheddar, a half pint of milk, a blanket from Orph's bed. He didn't go into the others' rooms now. He stuck to an area comprising the kitchen and half the sitting room, occasionally venturing up to the toilet. He slept in front of the TV, wrapped in his blanket. He stared at the items on the kitchen table and refrained from touching them once they had been used. He kept the kitchen gas fire on all the time. There was a pool of water on the floor around the fridge. The kitchen began to smell. Christmas passed.

Emma was the first back. She looked at the living room and kitchen. It was revolting. She didn't say anything, but made them both a cup of tea. The doorbell—Phil.

He stamped straight in. "What a bloody awful mess. What's going on? It stinks."

There was a slight silence, then Emma laughed. "Orph's been experimenting in housekeeping, haven't you?" Orph looked around the room blankly.

Phil smiled at Orph. "Want some experimental help in clearing up? Come on, I'll give you a hand." He propelled Orph to the sink. "You wash."

Emma went up to her room. She sat on the bed and looked round. It smelt faintly musty, but also of her perfume. Her hyacinths on the windowsill were poking healthily through the soil. She had put up deep red velvet curtains before Christmas, and the green leaves looked well against them. She liked her room. She chose a record and put it on her stereo.

Chapter 32

But something had a grip on her now. A premonition, clinching in with the steely cold, of something dying. She was a puppet, someone was going to pull the wrong string. Perhaps it was David. From time to time she considered ending the relationship. Although she did not ask him, she felt fairly certain that he was seeing someone else. Why don't I ask him? It was simple: because she didn't want to know. She was drawing in and into herself, he barely touched her now. At times a convulsive sentimental regret swept over her and she clung to him weeping, but she could not convince herself that it was real. He jarred on her.

They stayed at his place one Saturday night after a party. In the morning they made love then he bounced up, had a shower, bought Sunday papers and made breakfast, while she still hugged the draining warmth from the bed. When she finally went into the sitting room there was orange juice and real coffee and croissants and honey, and the *Sunday Times* and *Observer* spread across the sofa.

He handed her some coffee and waved at the papers by his side. "News or chat?"

"Um—chat, please."

He laughed. "I knew you'd say that. Women always do!" Emma bit her lip.

They ate breakfast slowly, amidst the rustling of pages. Emma was uncomfortable. It was an easy luxury which, for some reason, she was outside.

He looked up and smiled. "OK?"

"Mmmnn." When she had finished her croissant she brushed the crumbs off her jeans. Looking for cigarettes, she went back to the bedroom, but stopped in the doorway. The curtains were still drawn. The wide bed was rumpled. The duvet had partly slipped off and the pillows had been squashed up against the wall at the bed head. Between pillows and duvet was the expanse of wrinkled blue sheet, with two little patches of white staining it. On the floor to the left lay a jumbled heap of both their clothes, removed in a hurry. Her handbag was thrown carelessly on a chair, the contents spilling out. It was like a scene from somebody's life. A picture in a gallery that you stare at with a voyeur's envy. Here they were, this is what happened, spell out the story from the evidence.

She sat carefully on the edge of the bed, so as not to

148

disturb any of those real wrinkles left by the real actions of two real people. She took cigarettes and lighter from her bag. I envy you, she told herself. Your life in this room. It was as pointless as envying somebody else. The bedside lamp was still on, as if the room waited for its inhabitants to return and resume their lives. He expected her to open the curtains to the grey daylight, switch off the glowing lamp, shake the pillows and tuck in the sheet. Pick up their clothes, turn them right side out and put hers in her bag. Cleanse the room of her presence, make it blank again. She didn't want to. She wanted it to stay. Like the calm glowing order of Dutch interiors; like Vuillard's crooked farmhouse kitchen— she longed to inhabit and be possessed by such a room. Rooms where lives were lived, objects known, their edges softened by intimate contact over time. Rooms which vibrated with their own identities. Seen by eyes that knew them, belonged to them.

Did the artists know that one day the courtyards would be empty of ladies in hoop skirts and little dogs, that the drawing rooms would lack musical instruments and players of them? That the checked tablecloth would be torn for dusters and the solid table find its way to the fire? Did they admit that from second to second the calm lives of those peaceful inhabitants could be shattered by death, disease, illicit passions?

She rose carefully and laid her cigarette packet down on the chair so that it again looked as if it had just fallen from her handbag. Walking carefully, as if the very air might be disturbed by her movements, she went back into the sitting room. He was on the floor, leaning on one elbow, head bowed over the newspaper. Another picture.

She tapped on the glass. "David?" Silence. "David?"

He looked up. "What's the matter?"

She hesitated. "Can I stay here today?"

He frowned. "What for?"

"I don't know—I just want to. It seems so odd." There

149

was a silence. "We're so disconnected." Pause. "A night here. A drink there. I'm—I don't feel real. I'd like to stay."

He closed the paper as if it were a box that he was putting the lid back on. "What d'you mean? We see a lot of each other."

"Yes—"

"Emma, we're not going to see any more of each other. You might as well be quite clear about that. We're busy people, we've both got our own lives to lead—we've both got separate lives."

"I haven't."

He stood up. "You're talking nonsense. Utter nonsense."

She could see he was getting angry. It's going to end today, she thought. Now.

"We don't own each other, Emma. You don't own me. Don't rely on me. We see each other when it's good, OK? That's enough. And don't cry. I can't stand it."

She wasn't going to. She was quite calm now, as if she had achieved her ghostly desire. He was angry, backing away. She had known it anyway. "All right," almost to soothe him, calm his ruffled feathers, "all right, I'm going."

He watched her get her things in silence. Don't say anything now though, don't say anything else. He followed her to the front door and held it open for her.

"OK, Emma?"

"Yes. Goodbye."

He hesitated, then he too said, "Goodbye then." She heard the door close softly behind her. She was relieved.

Chapter 33

David spent the day reading. At six o'clock he went into the kitchen and began to prepare a meal. Annabel was coming to dinner. He took the meat from the fridge and unwrapped it on to a plate. Two bright red slabs of steak stared up at him. From various parts of the kitchen he assembled garlic, fresh runner beans, aubergines, seasonings, saucepans. His face was set in a smile. Taking a clove of garlic he stripped it carefully with a sharp knife. He cut the naked white kernel in half, and grasped half between the ends of his stubby thumb and forefinger. Taking one thick drooping steak in his left hand he rubbed it slowly with the garlic, feeling the strong stretchy grain of the meat moving under the pressure he created. His nostrils widened to take in the mingled blood and garlic. He enjoyed cooking. He sliced the beans rapidly and accurately, allowing them to fly off the knife end into the saucepan. One or two fat pink inner beans he removed pickily from the pan. In their swelling pinkness they looked pregnant, ready to burst. He sliced the purple-black aubergines as precisely as a surgeon. Their resistant oily dark skins divided at the blade touch, revealing the pale yellow flesh within, the seeds and softness. He put them on a plate ready for frying. When it was all ready to cook he ran himself a bath and put new sheets on his bed.

He bathed slowly, looking down the length of his body as it hung, half-floating, in the water. Four long straight limbs lying relaxed in the water, supple with muscles and the knowledge of movement. A thickly built torso with working belly and lungs and heart, machine parts, running smoothly. A small delicate penis floating under the water like a drowned thing, feigning innocence. A head that could look down and say, I am self-contained. He dried his body lovingly, as if it were a new gift.

While the food was cooking he poured himself a half tumbler of whisky. He drew the curtains and switched on the lamp. It is surprising, but I am upset, he thought. His pain could find no expression. The lit room stood factually around him. His brain ran through the twists of the problem and found no answer. Dead ends. These women. At a point where they began to believe something like real affection existed between him and themselves, their own identities began to disintegrate like rotting fruit and they dropped, helpless and disgusting, into his lap. How could it be his fault? He was seized by the claustrophobia of being alive. Alive, in a cage of flesh and bones, trapped within the dreadful confines of his own knowledge and experience. Never able to leap beyond.

He reached for the whisky bottle set by the stereo and topped up his drink.

Chapter 34

"I'll come."

Phil turned to Emma. "You? Why?"

"Why not? The more the better, isn't it?"

"Sure, yeah, OK. Can you pay me now?" Emma went to find her purse and Phil added her name to the list of people who'd paid the coach fare to London. There was a demonstration on Saturday.

"Does Orph want to go?"

Phil nodded.

"Here, take for him out of this too." She gave Phil £10.

"Anyone else?" Phil sniggered. "Not really dear David's scene, is it?"

"Phil shut up." Alison's face was white with a red thumbprint on each cheekbone.

Phil wrote something on his paper then looked up, his face contorted with irritation. "Shut up yourself for Christ's sake."

Two coaches went. Phil rushed up and down organizing people and fitting in banners and collecting more money, and finally got into the second coach. Alison and Emma sat together in the first, with Orph behind them. People started to chant, and bottles and cans of beer were passed from seat to seat.

Alison shook her head. "I feel too old. It's like going on a school outing."

Emma nodded, staring out of the window. The land was flat and wintry grey, grey roads grey sky grey iron trees, grey river meandering through. The coach was a silly bubble of noise. People were shouting and laughing about how to protect themselves, showing off layers of clothes with newspaper stuffed between. "Do they think they're going for a fight?" Emma was contemptuous.

The coach took them to Edgware Road. In all directions Oxford Street, Edgware Road, Marble Arch, Park Lane and the park itself were dense with bodies, but the effect was strikingly different from an ordinary crowd. It shocked Emma to see so many so oddly similar, and to think that she might be as easily classified as they. Most were older than Emma and Alison, and many had young multicoloured children with wellies and hand-knitted mittens. Babies hung in pouches on people's backs or stomachs, like marsupials.

Alison laughed as Phil pushed into view. "Great, isn't it?" he said, and put his arm round her shoulder.

Like a gardener who's proud all his cabbages have come up, thought Emma. "You can see why the British textile industry is in decline," she said. They looked at her. She waved her arm towards the crowds. "Just look around you—it's all second-hand or third-world.

Oppressed peasants who make Peruvian jumpers must be doing a bomb!" Phil laughed generously and Emma was pleased, though she had intended it as a taunt against him. Orph stared in silence. He was wearing an old jumper of Phil's, hand-knitted and baggy with a mock-Fair Isle pattern on the front. Emma decided she would give him some money for a jumper.

Fighting up the underground steps more heads, bodies, legs came into view. The pavement was crammed. Traffic on Park Lane was crawling while streams of people flowed between the cars, joining the great sea of bodies that filled the park, stretching as far as the eye could see.

"It's amazing!" said Alison. She was intoxicated by the numbers, and some of her excitement even penetrated Emma's gloom. The power of so many people—the power! They crossed Park Lane. People were singing, shouting and milling about, laughing and smiling at total strangers. Phil led the way through the crowds. Emma could hear a tannoy, the voice patiently repeating itself. They heard the same sounds over and over, though they could not distinguish the words. The crowd seemed to be centred well away from the road, towards the middle of the park.

The view from the police helicopters chop-chop-chopping above was peaceful enough. The masses of people in the park were moving only slightly. Gradually from the myriad dots the march took shape, its body punctuated by stripes of banners. It was created simply by the density of the dots. The tired winter-green grass was a background to them. Bright sunlight lit the city. Windows of offices and hotels and cars glittered silver. Cars crawled infinitely slowly down Park Lane. From the little flying capsule of metal and plastic, encased in its own noise, the park and streets were as pretty and peaceful and silently slow-moving as a child's kaleidoscope, where the coloured crystals fall slowly into each new pattern. London. The crowds and sun gave it an air of holiday. And like kaleidoscope repeating patterns, dark lines of navy blue encircled groups of other colours, lined Park Lane, and demarcated the sides of the march monster. A line of motionless black vehicles stretched up one of the little streets to the left of Park Lane.

Phil flung himself into rapturous greetings with long-lost friends who were clustered under the NUS banner, while Alison and Emma smiled dazedly at everyone. Orph, unnoticed, detached himself from the group and wandered on down the side of the march. Groups were still slotting themselves in and waiting for friends to join them. The loudspeaker repeated tirelessly the order they should be in, and people who were cold and bored with greeting forgotten friends looked nervously backwards and forwards, checking their positions. There was a policeman standing every ten yards, facing inwards on the marchers. Orph passed one who was in laughing conversation with two girls. Others stood stoically, arms folded, staring in front of them or wandered from their positions to chat with their neighbours. The loudspeaker voice was becoming hoarse, and more insistent. The front of the march was beginning to move. Orph left the crowds and cut across the park which was littered with papers, cartons, tin cans. Isolated groups of people, twos and threes, stood now amongst the rubbish, but nearly everyone had joined the march. Bright yellow leaflets blew across the grass in handfuls. He went back under the iron trees to Speakers Corner. An old man in a fawn mackintosh was talking about God but no one was listening. A crowd of stragglers clustered round the ice-cream van near him, buying canned drinks. Orph moved down under the trees and positioned himself by the railings bordering Park Lane. Two policemen were holding back the traffic, and coming out of the log-jam of Marble Arch corner the trickle of marchers began to move more swiftly, like the front end of a worm surging forward from stationary fatness. The atmosphere was carnival. Laughingly, people adjusted to carrying the banners high, moving further apart and getting into step. Two women banged tambourines and started to chant. A group of punks came tumbling past, two boys young and very self-conscious in black leather trousers, festooned with chains looping round their waists and down their legs. A girl with them had a shaggy halo of electric pink hair and black-rimmed glazed eyes. A contingent of uniformed nurses followed them, dumpy-looking in their short skirts and flat shoes. They were unsmiling, purposeful, as if tackling an unpleasant part of their duties. The sound of raised voices came from the corner, and the flow of marchers ceased. The line of police shifted and cars slowly began to move down the outside lane.

Other people gathered by the railings near Orph began to mutter. "Bastards! They're breaking it up. Look—letting the fucking traffic through. They're breaking it up. It'll take hours, at that speed—people will drift away." Way back round the park those at the tail end of the march had not even begun to move. They stamped their feet in the cold and breathed out steam. At last the cars stopped and a new group of marchers burst forward. The police moved in like pincers on either side to prevent the march from becoming too wide. "Fucking pigs. We should have three lanes. Look what they're doing." The chop-chop-chop of the helicopter broke in on the other noises, as it moved slowly above Park Lane. Several marchers paused to raise and shake their fists at it. A hawker with a wide tray of badges moved up the march against the stream, and people clustered after him, eager to buy labels.

An officer who had been walking up scanning the marchers paused before Orph, blocking his view, and spoke swiftly into his walkie-talkie. Noise was coming. Driving very slowly, an open backed lorry with a group and loudspeakers balanced on the back. Their electrified voices rang out shrilly. The marchers following them danced along, laughing and joining in the song. The officer moved on, pausing to speak to each policeman on his way.

Orph left his post at the railings and began to walk down alongside the marchers but still in the park. People at the railings were waiting for their friends to march past so they could join them. There were several photographers hovering there too. A group of people emerged from a flashy hotel on the opposite side of the road and stood staring in amazement, clutching their thick fur coats to them. There were two women in the party, both with glossy black hair piled up above their carefully made-up faces. People passing shouted at them and they recoiled fastidiously and ducked to enter the waiting taxi. A policeman stopped the marchers for them and waved them out into the road. There were fewer smiling faces now. The marchers conversed in low voices, looking forward to the thin straggle that the often-broken march had become and back to the milling crowds still waiting to move in Hyde Park. From among the slogan-chants of various groups emerged a deeper ground swell, a beat like the breathing of the march. Only one word was distinguishable, stressed: "Out! ... Out! ... Out!" Policemen stood straight-backed, eyes narrowed, staring into the march or over the heads of the marchers.

Orph moved on, walking faster than the marchers, past photographers, police, idle spectators, past the glittering revolving doors of smart hotels, past trails of rubbish left by the marchers. Suddenly there was a shout and two police darted into the body of the march. The marchers coming behind piled up and gathered round. Some who had gone on ahead ran back to see what was happening. Within seconds there was a mob blocking the entire width of Park Lane, with police tearing people away from the outside and pushing their way in. A siren raised its wail and the black van at the front of the waiting queue peeled off and crept round the corner into Park Lane. It moved along slowly, accompanied by shouts and boos from the excited marchers. At Speakers Corner the police cut off the march, holding back the traffic also, until the way was cleared.

Orph leaned against a tree watching the vigorously pushing backs and arms. People were shouting, someone was screaming. A trickle of people were detached from the mob by the police and packed on their way towards Piccadilly. Then the crowd split and three policemen ran out, holding/dragging between them a figure whose face was smeared with blood. The doors of the van opened and closed on them. People turned in confusion; some of them, not knowing what had happened, found their friends and walked on. A smaller group gathered quickly around the black maria, shouting and gesticulating. The police answered them in lower voices. One of the arguing marchers took a quick step forward then froze, right arm half-raised. The others crowded in behind him, pushing him closer to the police. Suddenly he turned, snarling, to them and as he did so two policemen stepped forward and took each arm. An ultimatum was delivered to the others. Against the crowd and helicopter noises Orph heard that silence, of fear and hesitation, as they glanced at each other. The man who was pinioned by police shouted something angrily and a woman joined in his cry, while the others fell back. The police took the woman who had shouted. The van doors were opened again and the two people shoved inside. The engine revved and the van moved off quickly.

The little group who had confronted it stood watching it go, then turned helplessly to one another. They drifted back into the body of the march, which absorbed them easily as if nothing had happened. That section passed by and its passing was punctuated by a flow of traffic, and then the next section came on.

Alison, Phil and Emma were under the next banner. Orph jumped over the railing and joined them, his arrival as unnoticed as his departure had been. They were complaining about the police.

Emma spoke with the indignant outrage of a respectable citizen who suddenly finds she's been conned. "How dare they! How dare they!" A rumour had filtered back about someone a group of police had attacked, dragged along the ground and kicked.

Phil was shaking his head sceptically. "I doubt it somehow, I doubt it. They may be nasty, but they're not stupid. They'd have a riot on their hands—" Orph walked silently beside Phil, near the kerb.

"But look how they're treating people. Look how it feels now, compared to before—" Emma gestured around her.

Phil nodded. "Well, what d'you expect? Of course, this is all new to you, isn't it? You've never seen our mighty police force in action before!" Emma was snubbed and did not reply, but the atmosphere of the march made an impression on her. There was anger and violence in the air, and it felt justified.

By the time the final sections of the march reached Trafalgar Square, the speakers had finished and gone and so had the leaders of the march. The circling helicopters watched the monster melt away into the dusk, disintegrating into groups and blobs that disappeared down subways and into doorways while the bright orange street-lamps flickered on all over London. It was gone without a fight—easily, as if afraid of the dark blue evening air.

Chapter 35

Emma began to take more notice of Orph's activities. The household regrouped into a tighter, more inward-looking circle. They ate at home nearly every night now, and quite often there was a group of Phil's friends as well. The kitchen became a special place. In the daytime it was bare, exposed, uncomfortable, but in the evening with the lamp turned to face the glowing red wall and half a dozen people round the table, with cigarette smoke coiling above them and smells of food and drink and the steady hiss of the gas fire, it was as secure as a cave against the wilderness. Condensation in thousands of drops on the window provided a curtain against the outside. From time to time a huge drop, becoming over full, would tremble and slither down into the drop beneath, and joining together the two made a dribbling run down the pane, clearing a little strip to outside view. But that soon misted over again. They were enclosed in that room, safe from everything outside. The conversations that took place there were different, insulated from the wariness that you needed outside. It was a room for friends, for conspirators.

Orph was always there. Sometimes he was reading one of the badly printed newspapers or pamphlets that Phil scattered like confetti wherever he went. Sometimes he was simply sitting staring at his hands; only rarely did it look as if he was listening to the talk. His face was expressionless, his spiky sandy hair standing up above it like fur. Sometimes his eyes would follow a conversation, moving to each speaker's face as if he were watching a silent movie, waiting for some explanation. Alison moved round the kitchen, providing platefuls of food,

160

cups of tea, rising to get the salt, to place the butter in front of Phil, to pause affectionately with her hand on his shoulder. He never acknowledged her publicly. Always there was a half-frozen expression on her face, something that could not be warmth and so was wistfulness, her desire to please. She looked too often at his face, moving purposely so that she brushed against him, aware of his needs before he was himself. He was absorbed in his own ideas and only irritated by her closeness when he noticed it or it intruded on what he was doing.

"For God's sake Alison, sit down and stop fussing. Nobody wants any more, do they?" He didn't give time for an answer, turning back quickly to his conversation with Steve. "So he reckons that with a bit of a push we could get most of them out within a week?"

Steve, who wore a striped blue woolly hat pulled so far down it nearly met his beard, nodded.

"Yeh—OK. Well, what we need to do is get some leaflets run off—a hundred or so—and distribute them at the factory gates tomorrow night and in the morning. Nothing complicated—figures mainly—give them a breakdown of the redundancy offer, and a few recent statistics about unemployment. Most important thing really is to talk to 'em, get as many as we can dishing out leaflets and stopping them—" He talked fast, and white flecks of saliva gathered at the corners of his mouth. Emma found it repulsive.

He was talking about a small local factory where half the workforce were being made redundant. A shop steward had been sacked several weeks before the redundancy news. Phil and the others had originally become involved in an attempt to stir up a strike on his behalf, but they had met with an apathetic response. Since then good work had been done, according to Phil, building up contacts. They were really getting through to the workers now. Alison was sitting on the edge of her chair, her face tight, smoking rapidly and staring at the bowl of fruit. Emma broke up a lump of cigarette ash with a match stick until it was fine dust and began to draw her initials on it, making its edges into a circle, then a square.

"—we need more people. We need to saturate them as they come out of those gates. We need at least six leafletters who know what the fuck they're talking about and can—"

"There's a union meeting tonight." Ellis was very bashful; now he was bright red with the effort of that sentence. Emma wondered how long he had held it in his throat, formulated, waiting for the moment to slip it in.

"So?" Phil turned on him angrily.

"Well," apologetic, "wouldn't it be worth asking them?"

"*Students'* union?"

"Yes."

"Crap," said Phil viciously. He was becoming a good performer—they all looked up at his angry face, waiting in the pause he created for what he would say next. "You know damn well it would be a waste of time—I'd be lucky if they'd even put it on the agenda. You'd get nothing from them. Half of them don't even know what redundancy is, and the other half'd run a mile if they saw a worker." There was a silence. "OK. We need more people. Well, we haven't got them. Who's gonna write the leaflet?"

There was a pause then Steve said, "I will. But I need that article, the one you were talking about, from the *Morning Star*."

"Yeah, yeah, with the figures. OK, I'll walk home with you and get it then." Alison stiffened in her chair. She liked Phil to stay the night. He did not often stay. "Alison, if he brings it over here tomorrow morning and you type up a stencil for 11.30 you can bring it down to me in the Union and I'll get it run off."

162

"No." Alison's face was contorted as if parting with that syllable were parting with some portion of her own flesh.

The word barely checked him. He turned, half noticing, irritated. "What? I'll be in the bar, I'm meeting Alex."

"No."

"No what?"

"No I'm not typing it."

"Why?"

"I'm busy tomorrow. I've got to write an essay."

Everyone was watching Phil and he knew it. Slowly he raised his eyes to the ceiling, tilted back his head and began to laugh—a grating, humourless sound. Emma watched the Adam's apple in his throat jiggling up and down. When he'd finished laughing he shook his head slowly. "I don't believe it."

Alison's face was burning, anxiety and the knowledge that she would be misunderstood put a squeaking whine into her voice that was painful to listen to. "Phil, you're not fair, listen. It's just not fair. You talk about doing things—working together for it and all that—and look what happens. You're just using me. I'm the typist. It's just—like women used to make cups of tea. At political meetings, women made cups of tea. And now you do all the talking—and all the planning—and write the leaflets and have the ideas—and expect me to do the typing—the mindless work. It's not right. Why don't you type it? Why doesn't Ellis?"

Ellis turned red but had no chance to speak. Emma sat forward in her chair to see Alison's face. She knew it wasn't simply what Alison was saying that was important. Alison was making a bid for Phil's attention by opposing him. She was trying to change the basis of the relationship somewhere, so that he would look at her with respect—well, so that he would look at her. She would be better off without him, thought Emma.

He leant forward, putting his elbows on the table, exaggerated speech and gestures as if she were simple-minded. "My dear Alison, the reasons are perfectly simple. I quite agree, it would be very nice, it would be perfectly delightful, indeed, if you had an idea—or if you planned something or wrote something. Likewise, it would be useful if I could type. But as it happens, I don't. And as it happens, you don't have any ideas—do you? Do you? I'm sorry, have I been missing something? Have I been sitting here talking while at the end of the table there great plans and ideas have been languishing unheard? I'm sorry Alison. Tell us your ideas. What do you think we should do?"

Alison's lips drew back into a thin straight line, as if sewn. After a second she pushed her chair back sharply and it fell over backwards making a loud noise. "I'm going to bed."

They listened to her going up the stairs. Phil slumped his head over his folded arms. "Christ. What's the matter with her?" He wasn't asking though. He's not interested, Emma thought. Wait for it. Yes. He turned to her. "What about—"

"No." He had known what she would say.

"Why not?"

Emma hesitated. "What's the point of it, Phil?"

"Of typing?" He put outrage into his voice, ready to bulldoze ahead.

"No. Behind all this. Look—just explain it to me. The factory's losing money. So they're going to make people redundant. So that they can carry on employing at least fifty. So you want them to go on strike. And if they go on strike, they lose the orders and contracts they've got for making things and the factory loses even more money, and ends up closing down. So everybody's made redundant. And that's fifty less jobs still—"

He ran his hands through his hair, vigorously, till it stood on end. "The point, dear Emma, is that if you lie down and take the shit, they'll shovel more on top of you. The point is that no matter how they explain their losses and needs and reasons to the press, it still so happens that the directors and shareholders continue to rake in a tidy fat profit while the workers work their balls off to be allowed to be underpaid in a shitty job. The point is that it doesn't even matter what happens to this fucking factory—I don't care if it closes tomorrow—the point is that they should learn what's being done to them and they should start creating hell about it. What's going to happen—all over England—it'll happen—is that this fucking system's going to break down. It's up to people like us to get into factories—to tell them what's happening—to show them how they're being treated—to fill them with rage, till the whole fucking country's in an uproar and the fat cats have to notice, nothing works anymore, no transport, no goods, no imports and exports—chaos—that's the point—make chaos, till the whole rotten barrel cracks apart at the seams and we can start again." He paused staring at her. "You're like a pair of fucking ostriches, you and Alison. Ask Orph! He knows."

Emma glanced at Orph. It was unheard of for him to be dragged into such an argument.

But Phil steamrolled on. "He knows what it's like out there, he's been traipsing round after jobs in some of these shitty places, he knows what people put up with. But no, you don't even look under your bloody noses, just lift them daintily a little higher in the air and 'la-di-dah, I've got to write my essay on romantic love' or whatever the fuck it is." She opened her mouth but he had started again. "Weren't you *there* on that march in London? Couldn't you *see*? Don't you ever read the papers? Look!" He snatched a paper from the heap on the fridge and jabbed at the front page with his index finger. "Look, just read the headlines here—'500 more jobs lost in Liverpool'. Here—'Police chief calls for stronger laws on pickets; Boy, 9, shot in Londonderry night of riots'—look that's on one fucking page—and again—'Savage housing cuts'. How can you ignore it? It's all part of the same thing. Are you *blind*?"

"Stop shouting, stop treating me like a moron, for Christ's sake, Phil!" She was trembling with anger. "All right, yes, no, I'm not blind, I can see what's happening. But Alison's right. That's what *you* think, it's what *you* see—and because you do, you expect us all to rush about and do what you say—and you don't treat us like equals, you treat us like tame morons and give us little tasks to do to help carry out your great ideas—"

"They're not my fucking ideas, they're what's happening in the world around you, that you're too short-sighted to bloody see—" He stopped speaking abruptly, as if he'd run out of words.

She stared at the table top, waiting for the heat to drain from her face. "You've still got no right to treat people like that. You assume you're right and everyone else is wrong. You set yourself above us." She paused, but he said nothing. She felt the four of them were looking down on her. Even Orph. Trying to move quietly, without looking at any of them again, she went out of the kitchen.

She went into her room but she was still so angry that it was pointless to go to bed. She should go and see Alison, but she didn't want to. What was the point of comforting her? She'd be better off without him. Why should he expect her to be something she wasn't? What right had he got? She stood on the landing and listened. They were talking, in the kitchen. She heard Orph's voice, though she couldn't tell what he was saying. Phil had really sucked him in. She found herself resenting it. That wasn't particularly fair, after all it was better than him watching TV all the time. But it made her angry too. All part of Phil's "holier than thou". He could see what was wrong with the world and do something about it,

166

while she merely worked for a silly degree. *He* could befriend Orph and give him a worthwhile interest, whereas she had merely · dragged him into an incompatible household and left him to rot.

On an impulse she opened Orph's door and went in. She hadn't been in there for a long time. It was different. There was still the same airless dirty feel about it, but it was no longer so bare. There was a heap of papers lying by the bed. She went over and stirred them with her toe. They were all Phil-type publications, lefty newspapers and political pamphlets. Orph doesn't understand this sort of stuff, she thought. On the wall opposite the bed there were pictures from newspapers and magazines, raggedly cut out and stuck with sellotape. She peered at them. There didn't seem much rhyme or reason to them. There was one of a street with two burned-out cars on their sides—in Ireland, she guessed. There were a couple of some big march, seas of banners and a line of police. And some colour supplement pictures of a film about a boxer. A whole series of the hero fighting and blood-bespattered. Another, grainy grey of newsprint, showed a terrified woman about to be stabbed. Emma realized that it must be from a film review. The only factor they seemed to have in common was violence. As she turned away she ducked her head to see if the other magazines were still under the bed. They were. Well, at least he hadn't put *them* on the wall. Orph had turned into something quite unpleasant. And now he would do what Phil said, blindly...

But what was wrong with that? She was the one who was wrong. Who had done nothing for him. Who still did nothing.

When she went to bed she lay awake for hours, and her dream finally was of Phil and Orph together, fighting, spattered in the bright red blood of the film pictures.

167

Chapter 36

The picket line met at the factory gates at 6.30 each morning. It was cold and dark at six when Orph got up. He dressed quickly, putting on clothes that felt damp with chill. He went down from his room and straight outside without getting anything to eat or drink. The streets were deserted at that time, with the odd single car speeding through. Most houses were blank and black, windows indistinguishable. In a few, though, lights were on, or came on as Orph walked by. Behind closed curtains other people's lives, their beds and their risings and dressings, their early morning yawns and skins and smells, their privacy. Orph walked past the windows. The curtains were all drawn, he couldn't see in. A milk float passed him, ghostly silent in its motion. Birds waking squawked from the rooftops. As he turned the corner to the road approaching the factory, another person came into sight, a man trudging along in front of him, shapeless and dark with a thick coat and cap on. There was a dark cluster of men in front of the gate.

Orph joined them silently. One or two nodded at him, and Phil, arriving seconds later, slapped him on the back. "Hiya kid. How's it going?"

Orph looked at the ground and muttered "OK," and Phil moved on to talk to the other men. In the east the sky was turning a dramatic purple pink, and a thin band of cloud that lay low on the flat horizon was tinged with yellow. Colour began to bleed into the dark shapes on all sides. Green of leaves and grass emerged, a man's red scarf grew bright; pale colourless faces were tinged pink. The purple in the east was lightening, gradually an even wash of pink, smooth as an eggshell, pink as a watermelon, was spread over the entire eastern sky, and for a few moments the world was beautiful in the magical pink light. Men's faces glowed warmly. All colours intensified. A fine faint sprinkling of frost on leaves and walls suddenly sparkled. The sun came up, shone for a minute or two in the crack between earth and cloud, then slid up from the horizon and was masked by grey. Daylight. Already stale, merciless as fluorescent light. Men turned up their collars and stamped their feet.

Someone was talking of getting hold of a brazier so that there would be something to keep warm over on mornings like these.

Another laughed. "You expecting a good few mornings like this then? Be glad to see the end of it, me, I'm not about to start making it comfortable. Might get into a habit then, see." They laughed companionably, their steamy breath mingling in the air. Orph stood leaning against the gate post—with them, but outside their cheeriness.

One of them moved suddenly. "Ey up—we're off." Round the corner came the olive green bus that carried workers from outlying villages. They were the hard core of those resisting the strike. Slowly it approached the gate.

"Close up!" shouted Phil. The men moved awkwardly to form a line across the gateway. The bus stopped several yards from them, rattling and rumbling, clouds of exhaust belching out into the cold air.

The driver leaned out. "Out of the road!"

"This is a picket!" shouted a small man with fair hair and a red face.

The driver laughed shortly. "And these are workers."

"Scabs!" shouted someone else. "Scabs! Scum!" In the frosty air their shouts sounded thin and unconvincing. No one could hear properly over the noise of the bus.

Joe, a tall man from the centre of the line, stepped

169

forward and looked up at the driver. He spoke formally. "This factory is on strike. We ask these men not to go into the factory as blacklegs." Men in the bus leaned forward to hear. He saw their faces patchily through the dirty, dust-smeared windows. One man had his nose pressed flat against the glass and smiled idiotically as Joe caught his eye.

"Come on," said the driver, "you've done your bit, Joe." Stern-faced, Joe signalled to the men, who moved aside with relief, and the bus crawled past them. Those inside stared out.

The man next to Orph suddenly went taut. "Livey! You fucking bastard—look!"

From the general weary awkwardness of playing a silly game, a real spark of anger flared up. The men clustered together, voices raised. "Said he was with us—the bastard!"

"Wants to save his own neck—that's all!"

"That's what they all think—they'll be the ones to stay—we'll get the chop."

"They're right an' all. We've separated the sheep and goats nicely for 'em, haven't we?"

Joe cut in contemptuously, "That's exactly what they want you to think—and if everybody thought 'n' did that, those fuckers'd be sitting pretty would'n they? They'll chop you anyway mate, whether yer strikin' or not."

Voices rose in protest. "But we're making it easy, aren't we, we'll be the ones they pick on." "Those bastards, it's them we're fighting for!"

It was a discovery; slowly the men began to feel an astonishing hatred for those who went in on the bus every morning. Men who had been personal friends with bussers were particularly bitter. The unfairness of it was overwhelming. They were striking to protect jobs. Those bastards wouldn't join them, so *their* jobs would be safe. It dawned on them slowly, from a haziness and a humorous indifference to unions and politickings, it

170

dawned on them that they hated those men. Not the owners, but the bussers; the men who should have been with them but were too cowardly. The picket didn't grow. In fact it shrank—by day five there were only seven of them, and it had become routine to step aside for the bus and then turn after it with that sudden surge of pointless anger, to shout emptily across the factory yard. Most mornings, two policemen in a patrol car drove slowly past, but they did no more than glance at the handful of men.

Phil was furious. "It's not a picket, it's a fucking kids' tea party. It's laughable." He spilled his anger to Orph, best of all listeners, who never argued back. He was particularly incensed by the police, angry as a point of honour that they had not yet considered the picket serious enough to involve themselves in it. "Those bastards. They sit there and bloody laugh at us. They don't even have to get out of their car, they don't consider us worth bothering with. Bastards. Fucking pigs. We'll show them—we'll make it worth their while. I'd like to wipe the smiles off those faces, Orph—Jesus, I'd like to shock them and show them we mean business. I hate those faces, fat complacent pigs—too stupid to wonder whose side they're on. They're not bright, they're not well paid—too swollen-headed with the importance of being a big nasty policeman to realize they're being shat on too. God I'd like to show them."

By the sixth day the glamour of being a picket line at 6.30 in the morning had worn off entirely. The talk was bitter as they waited for the bus, collars turned up futilely against the driving rain. "Saw Thomas last night in the boozer. The cunt. Smiled as if butter wouldn't melt. Sent his wife over to say hello to mine. I asked her if he was getting us a round in, seeing as he's getting wages and some of us aren't." He laughed shortly. "Then I got it in the neck from my missus—why haven't I got as much sense as him, and why take it out on the poor woman anyway—talk about support, changes with the bloody wind." Others joined in. Their wives were against the strike. They were frightened. It was the bussers' fault. Orph stood close with them as they talked, inside the circle of anger and complaint.

After the bus had gone in, Phil called after Joe as he was marching away from the gates. It had taken him a while to conclude that Joe really didn't know what he was doing.

"What?" Joe didn't stop walking, and Phil had to run to catch up with him.

"This is hopeless. It's bloody useless."

Joe said nothing.

"Look, what's going to happen? They're drifting away already. Every morning we let the fucking bus in—we might as well stay in bed."

Joe stopped. "What d'you want to do?" he asked wearily.

"We've got to be more aggressive. We've got to stop the bus—what the bloody hell's the point of standing aside for them every morning, like a row of fucking butlers?"

Joe started to walk again, Phil side-stepping eagerly beside him. "You're going to stop a bus with six men and a boy who've never been involved in any action before."

"Well, either we do something or we give up—this is worse than useless." The police car, late this morning, drove quickly past them and through a huge puddle, showering them with muddy water. "Fucking wankers!" Phil hopped up and down, flapping water from his coat. "I bet they're killing themselves—"

Joe spoke evenly, interrupting him, "The only other thing we can do is call a mass picket."

"Well why don't you?"

"Because I'm not sure we'll get many takers."

"But even a few—and I could get a couple more students along—"

Joe winced. "I could spend a week trailing round and

172

get nowhere. They'll support us in principle—by the time I've been round to every convenor I can get hold of and spun them the sorry tale. And they'll call meetings and rant about support till kingdom come, just like our lot—then we'll be lucky if we get more than one bloke along from each place. And they'll be the militant loonies anyway."

"That's exactly what we want Joe. Militants—action—fireworks—something to *happen*."

Joe looked at him. "You're not dry behind the ears yet, lad." He lengthened his stride.

"When?" called Phil, stopping.

"Give me three days. Friday." He walked rapidly away.

Phil was delighted with his success. It seemed to him that Joe didn't have the confidence to push this into real confrontation—but he did have the men behind him. With Phil's help they could really put this dispute on the map—why not? Next stop flying pickets. He went back and told Orph gleefully that there would be fireworks on Friday.

There were twenty-seven men at the gates on Friday morning.

Phil was exuberant. "We're gonna get them today, boyo!" he told Orph. He made a clenched fist and punched it into his left palm. Orph nodded back with the ghost of a smile on his face. They stood in a noisy crowd in the gateway, Joe in the middle discussing tactics with three of the new men. Steve and Ellis arrived together and smiled at Orph without speaking. Conversations stopped dead at the sound of engines. Two police vans roared around the corner and stopped a hundred yards from the gates. In the sudden silence the men stared. The van doors opened and ten policemen emerged rapidly from each.

Joe swore. "I thought we'd kept it quiet." The

173

policemen moved towards them, and the newcomers amongst the men moved resignedly aside. The original pickets stood still, staring like rabbits.

"Move aside!" called a sergeant briskly. "Clear these gates." The men looked confusedly at Joe. He gave a slight shrug and stepped aside. They allowed themselves to be shepherded into two little huddles on either side of the gateway, penned in by a line of police. It was so sudden and efficient that they hardly knew what had happened.

Phil was at Joe's elbow. "What the fuck are they doing? Why did you let them move?"

Joe glanced at him contemptuously. "We're outnumbered, man."

The quiet was eerie; apart from the sergeant's brisk voice, the police didn't speak at all, and the men were cowed and awkward. Phil was furious. He longed for scenes like newsreel pickets where hordes of men, drunk with the power of their numbers, screamed and jeered at police, even when face to face with them. Here, it was pathetically small and intimate; it was embarrassing even to talk. The police stood in two silent lines, arms linked, as if they were about to execute a stately and formal dance. Their neat uniforms contrasted starkly with the men's shabby layers against the cold. Someone said, "They're coming," and there was a stirring amongst the two groups of men. They took their hands out of their pockets and moved forwards, craning their heads to watch the bus approaching. The newcomers to the picket, Joe's militants, moved right up behind the police, linking arms. Orph found himself pulled into it by Phil, who twisted his arm around Orph's elbow. To his left was the short fair man; he fumbled awkwardly for Orph's arm then grasped his hand as the bus drew level with the end of the police line. The sudden noise of the engine made it possible to talk again and the new pickets were shouting "Push! push!" The bus windows were steamed

174

up, but the passengers had wiped clear patches to look through. Their faces stared out nervously.

Someone yelled, "Get them!"

"Scabs!"

"Go home!"

"Cunts!"

Screams of rage broke from the men and they threw themselves against the police backs, forcing the channel they had cleared to close in slightly. The bus slowed. Instantly the police were unimportant, no more than an irritating fence which happened to be in the way. The men heaved against the solid blue backs, some butting with their heads, others reaching over to batter the sides of the bus or kicking at it under the policemen's arms, their fury all directed at the familiar faces behind the glass. The policemen were forced in so that they were only inches from the juddering rattling bus, and as the enraged pickets thumped its sides, the driver lost his nerve and stopped completely. For a moment there was nothing but screaming and hitting. Looking down, Orph could see Phil's foot kicking repeatedly at the policemen's legs. The fair-haired man's grip on his hand was tight and slippery with sweat. The engine revved ear-splittingly, the bus jolted forward and was past them in a fog of stinking exhaust. The line of police broke suddenly as the man in front of Phil twisted round sharply to grab him, and Orph went sprawling forward on to the ground. He scrambled to his feet and lunged after Phil—who was already being dragged away, bucking and kicking. "Fucking pigs!" Orph screamed shrilly, and one of the policemen holding Phil looked back coldly at him.

From behind, the short fair man grabbed hold of Orph's hand and pulled him back into the body of the crowd. "They won't let go of him for you!" he muttered, with a flicker of humour.

Finally the majority of the pickets were back against

175

the wall, looking as awkwardly uninvolved as they had at the start. The factory gates swung shut, the doors were slammed on the last of the arrests, and the remaining line of policemen walked quickly away without another glance, as if the men behind them were less than nothing.

Embarrassed and silent, the men watched them go then glanced at one another. Joe had been taken. And Phil. And three other men. They broke apart and went quickly towards their homes. Orph was among the last to move. He kicked at a piece of glass lying on the pavement, kicking it along at every step up to the corner of the street. Then he gave it a hard kick that sent it spinning into the air to land in someone's garden. Mechanically he tucked his shirt into his trousers and walked slowly homewards. His pale face was as expressionless as ever.

Chapter 37

That night he and Emma were alone for supper. Alison had gone down to the police station and was going on to see Steve. Emma questioned Orph nervously about what had happened, and he gave her a short, factual account. She felt guilty and ashamed, and spoke to him with the caution and respect that had been part of her approach to him a year ago, at the children's home.

When he had finished eating he went straight up to his room and sat on the end of the bed in the dark, looking out of the window. It was drizzling, but there was no wind, so the window was not even spattered. It was as if the rain was falling a very long way away; it pattered lightly on the roof and garden outside, giving the silence a dimension. Looking out to the right, it was possible to
176

see a small section of street beyond the gardens of the neighbouring houses. There was a street-lamp in the middle of it; on either side the wet street gleamed orange-black. The church bell tolled nine. Orph sat in more or less the same position for the next hour. During that time two pedestrians with a dog went down the street and three cars swished slowly past. The church bell tolled ten, and from downstairs the urgent theme music of the ten o'clock news and Big Ben's shorter, swifter strokes mingled oddly with it. A few minutes after ten, another pedestrian appeared. A tall one, with a strangely bell-shaped head. Orph leant forward intently, then ran down and out into the rain, leaving the front door slightly ajar behind him. He was in time to see the tall pedestrian—a man—slowly cross the shiny street at the junction and turn left out of sight. Orph looked up and down the empty dripping street then returned silently to his room.

The management sacked everyone who had been on strike. Those who had not continued as if nothing had happened. And so it was over, as pointless as if it had not been, leaving in its wake only a small group of embittered, impotent men talking endlessly of revenge as they queued in unemployment benefit offices.

Phil was released next morning, but charged with threatening behaviour. His case would come up in court in a month or so. He recounted vividly how they had been pushed around and insulted, and his arms and shoulders were covered with bruises to prove it.

"You can't prove it," said Alison knowingly, "they'll say you got them fighting on the picket line."

"I know," he spat and turned his interest to Orph. "What happened to you? I heard you yelling at that bastard, then I lost track of you."

Orph shrugged. "I was there," he said.

"Oh yeah, yeah, I know—lucky they didn't pick you up

too, the way you were going for them. What happened after we'd gone?"

"Nothing much. They just drove off. We stood around for a bit, then came back."

Phil nodded. "Bastards. Shit heads. They fucking walk over us."

For a couple of days he was very depressed, as if it had been a personal failure. He stayed with Alison, although they hardly seemed to speak, and was around the house in the daytime, when Orph was. He was full of bitterness for the factory workers. "Roll on the day when they've got nothing, when they're starving in the streets, 'cos then they'll have nothing to lose and they might even show some guts. Fucking wankers." Orph listened and nodded.

Emma, seeing Phil's bruises, and hearing Alison's furious account of how the police had told her to "run along now little lady" when she went down to see him on the night of his arrest, faltered in her tracks. Parts of her life were receding and going out of focus like a badly made film. The bright safe university world became wobbly and unreal. When Phil told them there was a demonstration in Lowfield the following Saturday, she automatically counted herself in. To have spent the afternoon in the quietly humming library instead would have been playing, mere make-believe. The fact that she was terrified by the physical danger involved made it that much more compelling. *That* was real. Writing essays belonged to a dream world, a bubble world so sweet and fragile it would burst any minute now. Phil's point of view was in urgent focus. As he described the reasons for the Lowfield demonstration, she could follow his arguments and see that it all fitted together. She had glimpsed it on the London march; now it was insistent and near to touch.

Lowfield was a run-down area to the east of the town.

High Victorian terraces cramped between decaying industrial sites. The houses were dilapidated, many of them bricked or boarded up, barricaded behind overgrown dusty privet hedges where balls of scrumpled up newspaper, empty cans and smashed milk bottles proliferated. The population was mainly West Indian. The big youth club in the area, held in a church annexe on the corner of one of the few roads which boasted trees, had been closed down the week before. Phil told them that the council had closed it because residents complained about noise, drunkenness and fighting on the premises and neighbouring streets. But the complaints emanated from, and were orchestrated by, the National Front. All the kids who attended the youth club were black. And there was nowhere else for them to go.

The plan was for the kids and youth workers to meet outside the youth club on Saturday and march from there to the town hall, where councillors were supposed to be treating some foreign twin-town bigwigs to lunch. They would deliver their protest to the councillors personally. Unless somebody tried to stop them.

"But there can't be many NF members round there, surely?" asked Alison. "Nearly everyone's black."

Phil sniffed at her naivety. "They'll come in from outside, from miles around. Don't need many, anyway— the amount of protection they'll get from the pigs— they'll outnumber us three to one. Bet you."

He was right. But the numbers on the kids' side were also much higher than he had predicted. Just as word had got round the NF supporters, so it had spread among anti-racist and left-wing groups. The scene was set for a battle. Alison, Emma and Orph went to Jessop Street together. Phil had gone earlier to meet friends. The whole neighbourhood was crackling. People stood in their doorways watching the street, arms folded. They waited in groups on corners, talking loudly and scrutinizing everyone who passed. There were police everywhere—parked in vans, talking into radios, patrolling the streets slowly in pairs. The air was electric. Near the club itself there was a feeling of anarchy—a lot of kids in their teens high and loud with excitement, shouting and laughing. Some were dancing to a transistor radio. They were nearly all black, and Emma was struck, and then immediately made guilty by, the sheer otherness of them. They looked so strange—like cattle, she thought, the same big prominent bones and swinging movements. They wore clothes as if they were decorations, all bright bits of things, sparkling crimson, yellow, bright green—the girls with tiny shiny plaits bristling all over their heads. She was frightened because they were so different, and felt she must be an obvious target for their dislike, being small and twitchy, pale and drab. The presence of Alison and Orph and, up front, Phil and a few other whites, was so diluted that it was comfortless.

They crowded in around her, overbearingly loud, and she began to panic. It was impossible to see ahead—or even out at the side—just a thick press of bodies, but she had to go along with it now. There was no escape. From a distance at the back of her head she watched the disconnected sections of newsreel film her eyes relayed. There was no commentary to make sense of it. It needed editing. Close-ups of backs and walls, sudden patches of black, faces and bodies appearing quickly and factually, undifferentiated in importance—long shots of a mass of heads or, sideways, a mass of legs, surging forwards. A white youth with a loud-hailer turned back to encourage the crowd, open mouth snarling. A full police coach in the first side street. A black man and a woman with a scarf on her head leaning out of an upstairs window with astonished faces. Shouts. The blare of a radio. Car horns. A group of kids pushing past them, bodies tilted eagerly forward, necks outstretched to see over the heads—thick

180

and dusty-dull as old rags, the dreadlocks of two youths in front—a policeman's scared face sideways through the crowd, speaking to his walkie talkie—shouting—coming together in a chorus of recognition, and sudden acceleration forwards—Orph breaking into a run—jerky now, the camera hand-held by a cameraman on the run—everyone running, sweat, panting, shouts and screams up ahead—a green sweater—the whole movement of the group faltering like water rushing up against a dam—coming up close behind backs and necks, more bodies pressing close behind— a shoulder with a white nylon shirt sticking to it—two arms lashing out sideways and up, hands grabbing, as a girl falls—blue uniforms pushing in from the sides, dragging people out—dense tangle of limbs ahead, screams and thuds—a glimpse of Phil, yards away, through plunging heads, waving them on—hair and sweating skin close—a shiny brown bottle in a white hand going up against the sky coming down fast—another long shot through a gap, to solid dark blue-black—a backdrop to all the tangle of bodies—an inflexible wave arrested there—blocking— faces turning—wide brown nostrils flared in horse-like horror with brightly red blood flowing—white eyes black skin mouth stretched open, a noise not a scream— noise—a stick long grey thing rising in air and coming down with a crunch... that stops all a second—keep away not a stick—don't look—disintegrating now not even faces—a hand flailing, and eye screwed up tight close, crooked mouth, brown cheek skin stretched taut— white teeth in pink cavern, hand dabbing, unbelieving light, on top of hair—blood telling fingers raised to check—flying through the air—ducking—lips snarled back, throat streaming noise—feet can't walk and now at the mercy to be pushed this way that way up against dark blue and going down, darker—white hand grasping on blue cloth, sudden shot of pavement a square foot of it clear and normal grey—up again across navy which

181

suddenly wrinkles and swivels with flashing lights down to grab—sky, white clouded, fringed with movement and noise—white mottled sky—pain arm sharp spinning round fast taste of vomit—black.

Chapter 38

As the group of kids and their supporters surged forward from the corner where they had congregated, police formed a double line sealing off the side street where a handful of white youths with cropped hair and black jackets jostled and shouted. Heading down Jessop Street, the leaders of the main demonstration, scenting the enemy, lunged off up the side street and clashed head on with the police. Who swiftly experienced difficulties. They were attacked from both sides and the pressure of bodies in the narrow street made it virtually impossible for reinforcements to break through. The row facing the National Front attempted to force them back, and their ranks were quickly broken. Fresh men hauled their way through the demonstrators, who were being dragged back wholesale. Police had sealed off the Jessop Street end of the street and were succeeding in dispersing the mass of demonstrators, although running fights were developing over a wider area. Orph, who was very near the front when they ran up (or, more accurately, were pushed up by the force of bodies behind) against the solid line of policemen, went down near the wall and didn't gain his feet for several minutes. When he did claw his way up it was to see Emma pushed violently against a policeman's back, grabbing at his uniform and crumpling. He saw clearly that another policeman caught her arm and twisted it behind her back and up to level with her head. He saw the first one take her other arm. He watched them start to drag her backwards.

Suddenly he was moving forwards from his position by the wall, screaming "No! No! Let go of her—" He bumped into a black girl who staggered back staring at his face in horror; he pushed her aside and pressed forwards. "You fuckers you're not taking her you're not taking—" He ran into a knot of people who were crowded round someone on the ground, lost his balance and fell heavily. By the time he was up again, Emma and the policemen were out of sight. He threaded his way back towards the end of the street. People were milling in all directions now, many of them hurt and helping each other. Orph was in time to see a black van move off from the corner of Jessop Street. When he got into Jessop Street itself, it was clearing rapidly. Clusters of policemen were gathering around their vans. Orph stood still for a moment, then went to the back of the youth club and sat on a step by the dustbins. There was the sound of vans and motorcycles moving off and of people shouting in the distance. Close to, the silence became vivid. Dusk was gathering. A lamp at the corner of the building came on and shone on the dusty leaves of the privet bush growing behind the dustbins. Orph, sitting on the step with his knees drawn up, arms resting on them and head buried in his arms, began to cry.

Two little West Indian boys suddenly appeared at the side of the bush, and stood looking at him. After a couple of minutes he looked up, smearing his sleeve across his face. "Fuck off you black cunts."

They turned and ran quickly, the taller of the two was shouting "One of them here—Joseph—Joseph—one of them Nazi shit—Jo---oseph—"

Orph jumped up and ran round the other side of the building, then started down the street at a brisk walk, keeping right in by the shadow of the houses. Four policemen who were talking in the middle of the road glanced at him but didn't challenge him. The kid was

183

still shouting, behind the club, and someone else was shouting back.

It got dark very quickly. Orph cut down side streets, making a zig-zag course for the centre of town, and was soon well clear of the Jessop Street area.

When he arrived back at the house it was empty. No one had been back. He had not seen Alison or Phil since the demonstration started. He made himself a sandwich, then went upstairs and sat on the bed in his dim smelly room. He sat there for a long time.

The church clock tolled ten. Orph waited till the last sound had drained away, then went to the toilet and then into Emma's room. He closed the door behind him and stood still, leaning against it, for about a minute. At last he went downstairs, closing the front door quietly behind him. The sky was black. He went across the gravel flat-footed and slowly, making very little noise, and looked up and down the empty dark blue street. Then he moved back into the bushes growing by the side wall and squatted down amongst them, completely screened by their black shadows. In his hand was a half brick which he had picked up from the flowerbed border.

Very soon came the sound of footsteps approaching. A measured, regular tread, not heavy, sounding clearly on two notes, tap-tap, like a child's wooden hammer. The heel then the sole of a stiff boot hitting the pavement. The silhouette of a thin man with a curiously elongated head moved past the end of the driveway and Orph stood up. He took two long strides along the flowerbed, avoiding the noisy gravel, and was on to the pavement. His feet in their rubber-soled baseball boots made no sound. The man stopped just the other side of the street lamp. Orph saw that his head was tilted right back. He was looking for stars. He made a snuffling noise in the back of his throat and brought out his white handkerchief. The sound of him blowing his nose filled

184

the quiet street. He stopped again, to put his handkerchief away and stare into a parked car. Very close to him now, Orph hesitated for a fraction of a second, weighing the brick in his right hand. Two paces behind the man, he twisted his body to the right to give the blow extra impetus, then flailed leftwards with both arms. The left, fractionally before the right, knocked the helmet forward over the face. The right, with the brick, connected with the back of the skull. The man gave a strangled little cough, like a polite churchgoer with a frog in his throat, and lurched forwards onto the car bonnet, his hands clenching and slipping on the shiny metal. Bending over him, Orph struck him again on the side of the head, hard. Without a sound the man slumped on down to the ground, crumpling in upon himself.

Orph glanced up and down the street. There was no movement. In the houses all the curtains were drawn. He could see the flickering light and shadows of a TV clearly through the thin curtains in the nearest house. He slid the brick under the car, giving it a little kick to get it out of sight. Then he grasped the policeman's wrists and straightened up to drag him backwards. For a moment the dead weight of the body did not give at all, and Orph strained backwards, using his whole bodyweight. Then the undignified heap which the police constable made on the pavement disentangled, the shapeless lump beyond the arms became a stretched-out torso and two legs which trailed behind. The blob of the helmet wobbled sideways and detached itself completely from the head. It rolled a couple of feet towards the gutter, was stopped by an uneven paving stone, rocked backwards and forwards twice and became quite still. Orph heaved the body out of the area directly illuminated by the street-lamp, dropped the wrists and straightened, breathing heavily. There was the sound of a car. He waited to see which way it would turn at the junction, and stepped smartly back amongst the bushes in the drive. The headlights moved along the dark street, pushing their pyramids of light in front of them, not coming near Orph or the dark shape by the wall. Orph kept his eyes on the helmet, which lay enormous and tell-tale, right under the street-lamp. The car passed without slowing. He watched its red eyes disappear backwards down the street, then slipped out and scooped up the helmet. With both hands he rammed it deep into the yellow litter bin which was fixed to the lamp post.

He dragged the body on towards the driveway. The policeman's feet and clothes made a loud noise as they moved along. The edges of the soles of his boots scraped along the pavement and clicked at every joint between paving stones. The stuff of his uniform rustled and rattled and made ripping sounds. Orph stopped again, half-bent—breathed deeply, then lurched the last few yards in a staggering backwards run, getting the body in skew-whiff on to the gravel. Two cars went past, their lights just reached to the pavement's far edge. Orph was safe in the darkness beyond. He looked down at the heap at his feet. Nothing in the dark shape was distinct except the pale bare face, and two white skinny forearms exposed like the legs of a chicken where the sleeves had dragged down towards the shoulders. Orph lifted the left arm to look at the watch on it—10.15—then dropped it like a piece of litter. He crunched across the gravel and unlocked the front door, pushing it open. Then he dragged the body across the gravel, making a noise like an avalanche, and hauled it up over the doorstep. When he dropped the wrists and went to close the door, it wouldn't shut because the man's legs were still in the way. Orph bundled them roughly aside, switched on the light and leaned against the wall, breathing heavily, looking at his prize. The man lay like a rag doll. The backs of his trousers were ragged and filthy where they had dragged over the pavement. A patch of hair on the back of his head was matted with blood. But it seemed to have dried already. The face was young, under thirty, with blemishes in the skin around the mouth, as if he had eaten something he was allergic to or shaved too closely. His hair was short and thin, and at the front it had all flopped over to one side of his head.

Orph rolled his head back against the wall, eying the stairs. Then he grasped the wrists again and started up backwards, heaving the dead weight one step at a time, gasping rhythmically. He did not pause at the top but went straight on to his room. The carpet ruckled up under the body as they crossed the doorsill but Orph kept on pulling, so that half the floor was exposed by the time the body was fully in the room. He rolled it over and pulled the carpet straight. Then he went to Emma's room and took four of her long Indian scarves from the wardrobe. He bound the policeman's arms behind his back, tying the wrists tightly together, and then he bound the feet. Suddenly he bent and put his ear close to the man's lips, and crouched motionless for several seconds, listening. He used one more scarf as a gag, and another as a blindfold. He tied his own scarf (formerly Phil's) tightly around the knees. He locked his door, sat back on the bed and lit a cigarette.

Gradually his face resumed its normal pallid colouring. He kept his eyes on the policeman as he smoked. The man lay on his side, trussed like a chicken, blindfolded face towards the bed. After taking a last drag from his cigarette, Orph placed it upright on the windowsill, alongside a row of similarly upright stubs each balancing a fragile tower of ash. He pulled the curtains wide open and stared at the black window for a moment. Then he went and switched off the light. When he moved back to the window, outside gradually became distinct— the black outline of neighbouring houses and a tree, besides the pinpoints of light in other windows and from street-lamps. The lower sky glowed a dull orange, the

187

colour of all the street-lamps. Above the orange the sky was opaque black, impermeable as brick.

Orph stopped above the trussed man and listened again, then went silently across the dark room and out of the door. He locked it from the outside. The house was dark. He went down to the kitchen, turning the light on after he had shut the door. Quietly he pulled out the cutlery drawer and picked up the carving knife. It was a heavy, old-fashioned one, the blade dark and stained, sharpened away to a dagger point at the end. When he ran his thumb along it it made a dent in the pad of skin. Taking up the knife sharpener he began to sharpen it, hitting the sharpener harshly with the blade at each contact, so that it clang-shrieked. He tested it again, then continued sharpening. The last time he tested it he only needed to hold it near his thumb for the skin to part and a thin line of red rush to meet the blade edge. He put his thumb in his mouth.

Back in his room he did not switch the light on, but carefully locked the door and laid the knife on his pillow before settling himself on the bed. The policeman was a dark shape with a pale oval blob of a head. He had not moved at all. Orph lit another cigarette and smoked quietly in the dark.

After a while there was the sound of voices outside, and then a key in the front door. Voices in the hall. Alison and Phil. A crack of light showed under the door as the landing light was switched on, and someone ran upstairs.

There was a light knock on Orph's door, and Phil's voice, "Orph? Orph? Are you there?" then Alison calling from downstairs,

"Phil, he must be back, the kitchen light's on," and the doorknob was cautiously turned.

"Locked. He's probably asleep," came Phil's quietened voice, and footsteps receded down the stairs. Their voices

188

murmured for some time downstairs, but the words were indistinguishable. Then they came out into the hall again and Phil said, "I wouldn't be able to sleep anyway—and I might be able to do something. Look, I'll ring you if anything happens. Otherwise, you try and get some sleep, and I'll be back later on—OK?" Alison's reply was inaudible. The door opened then closed slowly and her footsteps came upstairs. The landing light went off and Alison's bedroom door closed. The stairs creaked and settled, and the house was silent.

Chapter 39

Orph sat as still as his captive lay, but he was wide awake. He kept his eyes on the window and the small section of street that was visible if you sat sideways on the bed with your head pressed against the wall. Soon after Alison had gone to bed a police car moved across that patch of street, driving very slowly. A few minutes later it came back again, going the other way. Then the street was empty. Orph picked up the knife and moved to a crouching position beside the policeman, shaking him by the shoulder. The man's weight rolled back slightly and he gave a stifled groan. Orph shook him again and twitched at the blindfold so that it no longer covered the man's ears.

Bending close he whispered viciously, "Shut up, pig. One squeak and you're dead." The body shifted slightly, then suddenly went rigidly still. Orph bent to the ear again. "Did you hear that, pig?"

After a pause the head nodded once, rubbing up then down against the lino. On the downward movement the man groaned again. Orph's grip on his arm tightened and he was silent.

"Know what I've got in my hand?" The man lay still. "Eh? Asked you a question, pig. Know what I've got in my hand?"

The head moved sideways fractionally.

"Feel." Orph knelt against the trussed body, reaching over the back to the tied wrists, and took hold of a finger between his own finger and thumb. The policeman's other hand rose with it like a bunch of bananas. Orph pressed the flat blade of the knife against the fleshy part of the finger. The man's arm twitched and the finger in Orph's grasp jerked away. Orph gripped the finger in the centre of his fist and bent it backwards from the palm. The man writhed and emitted a tiny noise which he instantly stifled. Orph bent the finger further back. "Yes. You got to do what I say—haven't you? I'll tell you what it is—see, it's a knife—" He bent closer to the ear. "It's sharp. Wanta feel?"

The head twitched, no.

"Don't you—wanta feel?"

The head moved rapidly from side to side as if it were trembling.

"D'you like knives? D'you like twisting people's arms, pig? That's what you pigs do, isn't it? Grab her arm—and twist it behind her back—twist it—" Orph lost his balance trying to twist the policeman's finger as he described the action. It would not go because the hands were tied together. Orph jabbed downwards with the knife, slashing the back of the right hand. The policeman's breathing got louder and quicker and his whole body began to shake. Orph rested his back against the side of the bed and watched him. The body shook rhythmically and the breathing was a quick succession of indrawn sniffs.

"Crying, pig?"

The policeman continued to shake and sniff.

Orph settled himself back comfortably with his feet drawn up in front of him, knees bent. "Pigs don't cry.

190

Stop it." The crying continued. Orph kicked him in the chest. "Stop."

The man froze.

Slowly Orph pulled back his foot. "You're scared. Fucking scared. Now you know what it's like. Don't know what's gonna happen—" he paused—"don't know where you are ... can't see ... can't move..." His voice faded out, then suddenly started up again. "Scared, aren't you. Wanta know what I'm going to do?"

He prodded the man with his foot, and the head nodded.

"Well, I'm not telling you, shit face."

The room was silent for several minutes, except for the cautious sound of the policeman's sniffled breathing. Orph prodded him again with his foot. "You're gonna die. That's what'll happen."

There was silence again and in it, the distant sound of a car. Orph raised himself to glance out of the window and squatted down again. He started to whisper again. "Yeah. Tell you what I'll do—I'll take this knife—and I'll, I'll slice you—bits off you—I'll chuck 'em out. Bits of you will get chopped off. Fingers—ears—nose ... I'll chop off your dick.

And I'll get my knife—and I'll stick it right—in the middle of your guts—and twist it round—to make a nice red hole—a deep one, yeah, like a cunt—a juicy red one..."

His whispering voice faded out into silence and all the policeman could hear was a rhythmical tapping sound—the flat of the blade against Orph's denim-covered knee. "D'you like cunts, pig?" Orph shifted abruptly. "You wanta know what I'm going to do?"

He waited a moment then went on. "I'm getting Emma back. That's what. And no one's gonna stop me. No fucker is. They'll have to come crawling on their fucking knees your lot."

Silence.

191

"Crawling on their knees and bring her back. She's going to stay here with me."

He spoke in bursts, pausing so long between phrases that his speech sounded completely disconnected. The policeman lay rigidly still, his legs trembling like taut wires. "She'll come to me. All of them ... can talk. Sitting there night after night—they can talk—'That's only Orph. He never says nothing.' But it's me that'll get her out. Me. Orph."

Silence.

"She'll come in with me then. She'll come—they'll bring her in the garden where I can see—all of them—and I'll tell them—PISS OFF

all your lot. She'll stand there—right—she'll look up at the window and, I'll say—'Are you glad?' And she'll look at me and say—'Thanks, Orph.'

"She'll come upstairs then and knock so I'll say 'Come in,' so she'll come in and close the door and stand there and look—I'll just be sitting here—just sitting with my dagger—she'll stare at me.

After a bit I'll say OK—and I'll slice the ties—sssst—I'll boot you out, you can go—she'll say, 'Orph—You saved me.'

'It's OK. Nothing to it.' And she'll say—'Orph—I—' She'll come up to me—"

There was a long silence. Suddenly he rammed the knife into the lino so that it stuck and trembled there. "Listening, pig?" he said viciously. "Listening?" He bent close over the policeman's ear. "Listen to me. Fuck. Shit. Wank. Fart. Cunt. Arse. Balls. Prick. Fuck. Fuck fuck fuck you pouf wanker fuck fuck fuck—" He sat back as suddenly, silent.

When he started to talk again his voice was calm. "She'll know I done it. None of them done it. Orph. It's only Orph. But it'll be me that done it.

Know what they all say, pig? Phil and them? Talk about pigs. Going to kill them all." His voice dropped.

192

"But I'm the first. I'll show them."

He got up and went to the window, leaned his forehead against it, looking out. "She asked me to come here. Before. She give me this room—see. Everyday—I seen her. Seen her with that bloke David—" He turned, talking to the policeman as if the bound man could see him, nod and understand. "OK—with that bloke David—I know—but I been here a long time. I can wait. It's like they don't see you, right, like you're not there—sitting there, walking along, nobody's bothered, only Orph—
but things happen. Right. Sometimes things happen. Like that picket."

He was talking more quickly now, leaning forward towards the man, watching his blindfolded head.
"He come up to me—Phil. 'You want to join the line?' I said 'OK something to do.' I went there and we seen the pigs sitting in their car. He told me what you do then—he said 'they're out to get us—they'll try and smash it up and put us away right,' he said, 'us and them—you've got to remember it, Orph.'
OK, us and them—'you're with us, Orph, in the picket—we'll fight them bastards—' Then they shout, 'They're coming'—everybody's nothing, all over the place and he shouts 'Get them!'"

He paused and turned back to the window.
"We're all together pushing—all together. It was funny, that bloke's hand—was wet, it was hot...
All holding on—all the line
together,
and it come nearer—all screaming and yelling noise of the engine—it stinks—all pushing together—closer and closer—
you can't stop us—the fucking pigs! Smashed it. You cunts—smashed it—they got him—fucking pigs broke it all up—took them away—
everybody's nothing again—" He stood still, in silence.

After a long time he moved abruptly from the window and sat beside the policeman again, leaning against the bed. "This time they won't. I'm going to win. They'll say *you*, Orph, you're with us! It was you what done it. Well done, Orph. And she won't say it's only Orph—I'll be something—better'n them—she'll see, she will..."

Slowly he reached towards the policeman with his right hand and very gently brushed the limp hair back from the forehead. "She will. Still scared?" The man didn't move. Leaning closer, Orph whispered, "You still scared?" The head moved slightly, neither yes nor no.

"Here." Fumblingly, Orph undid the blindfold. The policeman's blue watery eyes blinked and focused on him. Orph leaned forward and patted the man's chest; the eyes widened fearfully, but Orph wasn't looking at him. He opened the policeman's breast pocket and drew out his note pad and pen. "Kidnap—see? Gotta do my demands." He stared at the page for a few moments then started to write slowly, resting the pad against his thigh. The watery blue eyes watched him.

When Orph seemed to have finished, the policeman shifted, wriggling slightly and nodding towards his feet. "What?" Orph put the pen down and watched him. The man squeezed his eyes together a couple of times, then shut them. Then there was a trickling sound.

Orph wrinkled his nose and jumped up. "You fucking pig," he whispered furiously. "You filthy fucking pig. Piss—pissing on the floor—you filthy cunt!" He kicked the man in the groin with all his strength. The body grunted and rolled sideways, limp. Orph stood over him for a moment then spat on his face. "Pig."

Chapter 40

Gradually the sky began to lighten. The black became dark blue, dark grey, luminous purple. A couple of birds started to cheep and clatter on the gutter. The room lightened. Stiffly, Orph stood up. He went to the toilet and then to Alison's room. Standing outside, he half-whispered, half-shouted her name.

She answered immediately, as if she had been listening out for him. "What? What's happened?"

"Get up. I wanta show you something."

There was a frenzied rustling noise from the bed and then the door opened. "What is it? It's the middle of the night." Her face was tight with fear.

"In my room." He led the way to his room and pushed the door so it swung open.

She stared blankly into the dim room. "What?" He pointed with his foot at the black outline on the floor. She took a quick step forward. "What is it? Orph, what have you—"

He grabbed her arm as she stepped forward, and yanked her back out of the doorway.

"Let me go—what are you—"

He pushed her against the wall and closed his bedroom door.

She stared at him. "Orph, what have you done?" Her whisper was so faint that he couldn't make out what she said.

"It's a pig. I've kidnapped him," he said in a normal voice.

"Ssssh—ssh—is he dead?"

Orph shook his head. "Listen," he said. She nodded. He dug in his pocket and showed her a piece of folded paper.

"That's for Emma. You've gotta ring the pigs and tell them—tell them I've kidnapped him—and I've got a knife. I'll damage him. They've gotta do everything I say. Tell them. If they don't—I'll kill him.' He pushed the note at her and went into his room.

Alison stood in the middle of the landing with the note in her hand. Suddenly the door opened again and a strangely familiar knife was brandished through the crack.

"See?"

She stepped back quickly and the door slammed shut again. Alison stumbled downstairs and collapsed into the chair by the phone. The house was silent. After a minute she picked up the phone and dialled a number. No one answered at the other end. She ran upstairs again and rattled Orph's door. "Orph, Orph!"

"What?"

"For God's sake Orph—let him go. You're crazy—you're going to get hurt—don't be so stupid, open the door!"

Orph's voice hissed from the other side—"Piss off."

She went slowly downstairs again and sat by the phone. Soon afterwards, Phil quietly let himself in.

She had barely started to explain it when he ran upstairs to Orph's room. "Orph," he rattled the handle, "Orph, come out—open the door."

Orph's voice came quietly from nearby; he must be directly on the other side. "No."

"Orph, let me talk to you. Look, come out a minute."

"No. Ring the police."

"But Orph—Alison said—"

"Yeah. I've got a pig in here. Kidnapped. I can't come out."

Phil leaned against the door in silence for a minute, then started to talk in a quiet, calm voice. "Listen, Orph, I know what you're trying to do—and it's pretty amazing. But you could really get into a bad mess over

196

this, Orph, they could put you away for a long time. Orph?"

"I'm going to get Emma freed."

"But Orph—Orph—look, they'll probably let her out today anyway. She was only on a demo, for God's sake—they'll let her out on bail and the worst she'll get in court is a fine. Orph? Orph? They're not going to keep her there."

No reply.

"Remember when I was arrested on the picket? It's the same thing. Like they did to me—keep me in overnight, then in the morning they let me go. I was back here by lunchtime, remember?"

No reply.

Phil thumped on the door. "Orph, for God's sake be sensible. Let him go now and I promise you nothing will happen to you. D'you hear?"

Silence.

"Look, the only thing that's going to make it worse for her is what you're doing. When they hear what you've done they probably will keep her in prison, they'll think she's done something serious. You'll get us all in trouble. ORPH! Open the bloody door!"

There was no sound from within the room. Orph must be standing completely still on the other side of the door.

"For Christ's sake!" Losing his temper, Phil hammered on the bedroom door with both fists. Alison watched from the bottom of the stairs. Phil stopped, breathless, and stood facing the door. "Orph, don't be an idiot. You'll get us all in trouble." Silence.

Alison crept upstairs. Phil stepped back to meet her and whispered, "D'you think we could break the door down?"

"Yes but the man's hurt—he's hurt, Phil, he's lying on the floor. Even if we get him out, what can we do with him? For all I know, he's dying—"

197

Suddenly Orph spoke, quite clearly. "Go and tell the pigs. If anyone tries to get in here, he's dead."

"Orph, you're crazy—"

"I mean it."

They argued in the kitchen for some time. Alison was in favour of calling the police immediately, Phil wanted to play for time. "If we can keep it quiet for long enough, Emma will be back anyway. Then she can sort him out."

"But he's insane. And what if the bloke's badly hurt? He was unconscious—he wasn't moving, Phil!"

"What's the time?" It was only 7.30. "There's no way she'll be back before 11, that's nearly four hours—"

"If we went and asked them—"

"That's what he wants us to do."

"Yes, but—yes." They sat in silence for a moment; the situation was absurd beyond belief.

Orph stood listening by his door. He couldn't hear anything. The policeman was conscious again, Orph had seen him shift position and heard him groan. He took no notice. He needed to piss but there was nowhere in the room to do it. He paced up and down a couple of times then screamed with all his might. "PHIL!"

There were scuttling footsteps, and Phil's voice on the other side of the door. "Yes. Orph? Orph?"

"Do what I said."

"Orph, let me in a minute please. Orph, you're being childish—you don't understand—"

After a pause, Orph said, "Fuck off."

Phil went slowly down again. Alison beckoned him into the front room, and pointed to the window. A police car, driving very slowly, was just disappearing from view. "I'm going to ring them."

Phil grimaced and turned away.

"Well what else can we do?"

Chapter 41

A police car arrived six minutes later. They had been at the end of the street. They'd already found the helmet. The dark uniformed men filled up the hall. Alison took them into the kitchen, and told them as much as she knew. "Where's his room?" asked the one in charge. He went upstairs and listened at the door. There was no sound. Softly he tried the handle. It was locked.

Orph's voice sounded very close. "Who's that?"

"It's the police. Open up please, sonny."

"No."

The chief inspector put his ear to the door. "Let me speak to the man you've got."

"No. Where's Emma?"

"Well how do I know he's alive? I must see him."

There was a sudden sound of frantic activity, a heavy piece of furniture being shifted across the doorway. When Orph spoke again his voice was muffled and breathless. "You can see through the window. Go in the garden."

Chief Inspector Pike ran downstairs into the back garden. The uncut grass was soaking and heavy with dew. He stepped back and looked up at the house. At the left hand window upstairs a boy's face was looking down. A pinched white face, with short sandy hair sticking up above it. "He's only a kid," Pike muttered to himself, and glanced along the row of sleeping houses where curtains were still drawn. He beckoned to his other men and they came out and stood with him, looking up. The boy's face disappeared, and a gagged head came into sight. It was low down. He must be crouching or sitting.

"Open the window," shouted the chief inspector. The

boy shook his head. They could barely make him out, through the white reflections of the clouds on the glass. "Could be anything," muttered the chief inspector. "The whole thing could be a bloody joke—could be a giant teddy he's got in there."

"But where's Neep?"

"Yes. Where's Neep?" Chief Inspector Pike stepped back again, shading his eyes against the glare of the light. Two heads were just visible, the white face of the boy and the other, gagged head. Pike sighed. Could be something or nothing, this. Some student joke probably. But mixed up with those demonstrators. They were a nasty crew. Found some lead piping on one. But the lad's mad—He could not take it in, first thing in the morning—bobby on the beat disappears—a hysterical girl says a boy in her house has kidnapped him; the lad demands freedom for a load of people who're about to be freed anyway, and stands there waiting for something to be done, with a knife at Neep's throat. It's 8 o'clock in the morning, people are having their cups of tea, wrapping themselves in dressing gowns and shuffling off to bathrooms up and down the street, turning on their radios and picking up babies from cots—it's impossible.

He turned to the man beside him. "Go up and tell him it's not good enough. We need to see Neep and hear him speak before we can start anything. Tell him to open the window."

The boy's face disappeared from the window. After a minute he came back, moved a catch and struggled to lift the sash. It was stuck. He hit it around the sides and managed to heave it halfway up.

It's not possible, Pike told himself. He's not got the strength. Are there two of them? Are they all in it? He cupped his hands to his mouth. Have all the neighbours out gawping soon. "Right, lad. I want to see my man and I want to hear him say he's all right."

Orph turned and the gagged head came into view clearly now.

"That you, Neep?" Chief Inspector Pike saw that it was. "Neep, you all right?" He saw the boy strike the other across the head and his blood suddenly ran cold.

Neep nodded.

The boy leaned forward through the window, holding out a long black knife. It looked like the family carver. Probably blunt. But Pike saw with dread that there was something wrong with the boy. Something strange about his face: he looked subnormal.

"He's all right," said the boy. His high voice carried clearly in the still morning air. "I got him. I got him—none of you could stop me. I crept up behind him—he's stupid, see, like all you pigs—I crept up behind him and hit him—easy. And I got him here. On my own. And now you're gonna do what I want. You're gonna do those demands or I'll stick him. With this. It's sharp."

There was a pause. "And I'm not scared of doing it." He turned suddenly and slapped Neep viciously across the face.

The chief inspector took a step forward, his fists clenching by his sides. "What's your name?"

The boy stared at him. "Dick."

"It's not!" escaped from Alison, who had run out after them. The chief inspector looked at her. "Orph," she said.

"Orf?"

"Yes."

"Right Orf. Listen carefully. I don't think you realize quite how serious this is." His heart sank as he spoke the useless words. The boy was a nutter. And this was going to be a fucking mess. A real fucking mess. "What I want you to do is to drop that knife down here to me and unlock your door so my men can come in. Stand to one side, no one'll hurt you. Let us get Constable Neep and then we can all sit down and have a talk about what it is you want. Right?"

201

Orph leant forward and hissed at them, "Fucking pigs. Fucking liars. I know what you do. You'll never get me—you're never gonna kick me around—never. Let Emma go. Let them all go. Now!" Gasping and heaving he struggled to shut the window, and yanked the gagged head out of sight.

The chief inspector talked to his men for a minute and they moved off in different directions around the house and garden. He took Alison and Phil into the kitchen and shut the door. "Right. Sit down. Now, what's he going to do?"

"I should get Emma here." Phil's voice was eager. "That's why he's done it. He thinks she needs freeing."

Pike glanced at his watch. "Is he all right in the head? How long have you known him?"

They looked at each other. "Yes—" both together, too quickly.

"Yes," Alison went on. "He's been here six months. Emma knew him before. He's all right, he's never done anything—"

"Right." Pike stood up. "He's under pressure now and he could crack anytime. I want my man out of there quickly and safely. We'll go into the details afterwards. Anyone else he'd listen to? Mother, girlfriend?" They shook their heads. "She was on this Lowfield business yesterday, was she? Second name?" He took a little radio from his pocket and spoke rapidly into it. "—and pull up at the corner. I want to speak to her before she comes in here. OK."

Alison suddenly pulled a piece of paper from her pocket. "This. I forgot—he gave it to me first thing this morning. It's for Emma." The chief inspector glanced at his watch again, and unfolded the piece of paper.

202

Chapter 42

TO EMMA emma i am ~~gowing~~ going to fre you. i got a pig ~~kin~~ kidnaped in my room and he carnt go til your fre tel them i got im last nite in the stret and i will damidg im if they dont what i say.

1 FREE YOU
2 AND THE OTHERS WAT THEY GOT ~~YISTE~~ YESTEDAY
3 PROMIS NEVER AREST ENY OF US FOR ENYTHING AGEN

sined orph.

ps. else its the nife for the pig

Emma looked up from the paper, towards the house a hundred yards down the street. The street was blocked off and there were two police cars outside. The tall policeman who had got into the car next to her started talking quickly. She watched the lines around his mouth appear and disappear as he talked. The driver was just staring forwards. As if he was deaf, she thought.

The policeman stopped talking, he was looking at her. She looked at the note again. She had never seen Orph's writing before. "Well?" he said.

"What—" her voice came out in a croaky whisper. She coughed to clear her throat. "What must I do?"

"He's in his room with my man, and he won't open the door. We're going to go into the garden—right? Out the back—" she was aware that he was speaking to her kindly. "...just talk to him naturally. You can see what he's asking for; right, tell him he's got what he wants, you're free, and nobody's going to get hurt. What he must do is drop the knife out the window, open the door and just sit there quietly while we get the injured man out.

He's het up, so try to keep him calm, just agree with him, let him know he's got what he wants—"

Emma twisted the note in her lap. "What—" Her voice was gone again. "What about this?" She pointed to the second of the three demands.

The man looked at her. "Yes, tell him it's all right—everything."

"But—" she folded the note up tightly. "What'll happen to him?"

The chief inspector glanced out of the window. "We'll talk about that afterwards. Just get him out, for starters. Are you ready?"

She nodded, and the car slid on towards the house. When she got out, it was terribly quiet and everything was very distinct and bright, as if the air had been taken away and there was nothing in between things. They went into the house. There were two policemen in the hall and two at the top of the stairs. They made it look small and dark. The policeman indicated the kitchen door. Alison and Phil were sitting in there. They stared at her without speaking. She noticed that Alison had been crying.

"Into the garden, then," said the tall policeman. They all stood up. "You two stay here," he told Alison and Phil. "I don't want anyone hurt."

Emma followed him out on to the wet grass. Lots of people had walked on it, it was all trampled down. The garden looked strange. There was something black by the fence. Then she saw that it was a policeman, crouching there. He held a gun. She tugged at the tall policeman's arm but he just nodded as if it was quite normal for there to be a man with a gun crouched by the fence. He took her to the middle of the lawn and turned her round. She looked up at the house, blinking in the light. Another man was crawling along the edge of the roof. All the windows reflected the clouds. The house was as calm as a house in a postcard, except for that odd figure edging along the top, crawling like a fly with its wings stuck together. She forgot why she was there.

The tall policeman stepped back, shading his eyes with his hands, scanning the house. Then he talked into his radio, to someone in the house. "Tell him we've got her outside. He'll have to open the window." Emma located Orph's window, and watched half a white cloud slide across it. It was tranquil and quiet. Even the birds had stopped singing.

A movement distracted her and she saw that people were leaning out of the upstairs windows, next door but one. As if they were watching a play, she thought. Then Orph's white face loomed into view at his window, like a fish coming to the side of a large murky tank. He leaned forward and heaved up the bottom half of the window.

"Orph!" She stepped forward. That's what the man had said; he was in his room, they would talk through the window. It must be true then. He stood a little back from the open window, white face with black features like the holes in a mask.

She remembered that face, he had come out of the kitchen a long time ago, when she was lying in the sun; he had been carrying a yellow plastic bag, and his toes sticking out the end of his sneakers. She stood still staring up.

The policeman was talking to her. With a jolt, she turned her attention to him. "Tell him. Go on."

"Orph—it's me. They've let me out, Orph."

The mask stared down, it could have been on a stick. Her mouth was dry. She had no words. The man on the roof was testing a rope he had tied to the thing in the middle. Now he leaned outwards and looked down to Orph's window.

She tried again. "Orph. I'm free. Because of you. They let me go."

He didn't move. They all stood in silence, as if the film had stopped.

205

At last she managed to break it, half turning her head to the policeman. "What must I say?"

The man's voice was brisk and irritated. "Tell him to come down for God's sake. Tell him to throw out the knife and open the door."

She watched Orph as the policeman spoke. He took a step nearer the window, as if to try and hear what the man was saying. She heard a sudden movement behind her, and shouted up, "Orph! Keep back—take care, they've got guns!" The mask retreated.

The policeman grabbed her elbow, pinching her. "Tell him to open the door," he said fiercely.

She saw that crocuses were coming up under the kitchen window, the yellow ones already blitzed by the birds. In her bedroom window was a pot of blue hyacinths. The air was bright, it seemed to tremble and shiver. "Orph," she said, calling to him now she could hardly see him. "Will you throw out the knife now and come down. You can see I'm here. It's all right."

The mouth in the mask moved. She couldn't hear. It moved again. "Tell them to go away."

"I—but Orph, they won't—until you let him go."

Silence.

The policeman touched her arm again. She opened her mouth and more words came out. "You can—they'll do everything you say. Your demands. Throw down the knife, Orph!" The man with the rope was beginning to come down the front of the house, very slowly. Transfixed, she watched him. Orph suddenly bent and vanished, then reappeared closer to the window, dragging another man by the shoulder. He pushed the man against the windowsill—he must be kneeling on the floor. Just his head and shoulders were visible. Orph stood behind him, above him. She saw that there was a black pointed thing clutched in his hand.

"Tell them—" the voice was high and childish "—tell them to go away."

She knew they wouldn't. The man with the rope was coming down, infinitely slowly and carefully—he stopped now at a signal from the chief inspector. "They won't, Orph. Please, throw it away. Let him go. They'll do it, Orph, your demands, what you said. Look, I'm free—"

The white mask stared at her, old and cynical. He opened his mouth once. "Liar."

"Orph—it'll be all right—just let him go—it'll be all right."

"LIAR!" he shouted. The mask cracked and there was a child up there crying, a betrayed child sobbing in the dark window space, words spilling out, "Liar—liar—they told you to say that—they brought you here—they told you—liars—all of you—liars—" his white face dark and broken into moving pieces. The chief inspector moved quickly and the man on the rope landed on the windowsill, instantly. The noise.

Emma saw it clearly, each detail crystal clear. He landed. Orph must have sensed his shadow, because he was crying, eyes screwed up—the man landed and there came a terrible scream from Orph's black mouth and the arm with the knife came down fast like a machine on to the gagged figure. And in the same instant of time, there was movement behind her and the noise—and the child's white face had vanished and the man was half in the window and everything rocked with the crashing of the shot

and though she had seen it all, every fraction of a second, her eyes hadn't caught that fraction—or hadn't registered it—the fraction which she realized later had been there right before her eyes—the vital fraction—when Orph's living crying face had been stopped by the bullet that pierced a small neat hole in his cheek and a big ragged one in the top of his skull, and splattered his brains and blood in an arc across the ceiling of his room.